Lions

THE BEAST

The doorbell sounded.

"Corinne!" she cried. "I'm so glad to see you. Hey, everybody, look who's here!"

Corinne hesitated in the doorway of the living room, smiling shyly as she surveyed the happy faces.

And then her smile faded. Her gaze had settled on Garth. Her eyes grew wide.

"No!" she shrieked, recoiling. "No!"

"Corinne!" Miranda cried. "What's happening?"

But she didn't seem to have heard. She backed away, still staring at Garth, her f ken. Then she ran out of the house

More heart-stopping Nightmares...

NIGHTMARES

THE BEAST

Cynthia Blair

Lions
An Imprint of HarperCollinsPublishers

First published in the USA in 1993 by
HarperCollins Publishers Inc.
First published in Great Britain in Lions in 1994
1 3 5 7 9 10 8 6 4 2

Lions is an imprint of HarperCollins Children's Books,
a division of HarperCollins Publishers Ltd, 77-85 Fulham Palace
Road, Hammersmith, London W6 8JB

Text copyright © 1993 by Daniel Weiss Associates, Inc. and Cynthia
Blair

ISBN 0 00 674915 1

The author asserts the moral right to be identified as the author of the
work.

Printed and bound in Great Britain
by HarperCollins Manufacturing Ltd, Glasgow

CHAPTER
1

A black cloud edged across the crescent moon, momentarily blocking its cold, eerie light. With the darkness came a chill, rising up in the damp air, an unwelcome reminder that autumn was quickly surrendering to the bleakness of winter. The powerful wolf paused in her race across the rugged terrain of the dense forest, suddenly alert.

Standing completely still, her sinewy muscles tensed, the animal peered through the ominous darkness that had settled over the woods lining the Oregon coast. The towering cedars, stately evergreens that reached up toward the blackened sky, loomed all around, their jagged peaks zigzagging across the horizon.

The wolf noted the beauty of the unspoiled woods surrounding her. Yet her appreciation lasted only a few moments. She sniffed the air, still vigilant as she stood with one paw poised in midair. Not for an instant did she forget that existing alongside the forest's magnificence was treachery. Her pointed ears were pricked, on the alert as she struggled to pick up any sights, sounds, or smells that meant immediate danger.

And then the cloud moved away. Satisfied that there was nothing to fear—no trap to avoid, no enemy to elude—the animal resumed her nocturnal prowl. Her strong limbs carried her across the forest floor in a swift, graceful motion. Easily she loped over jagged rocks and fallen trees, their bark rank with decay.

The other animals scattered, scurrying out of her path, seeking refuge under bushes or inside burrows. She knew they feared her. Not one of them was her equal.

Tonight, the wolf ruled the forest.

She luxuriated in the feeling of running unfettered, relished the sensations of racing through the forest. Her muscles were strong and seemingly tireless. With each stride she crossed a distance so large she felt as if she were flying. The icy wind whistled through her coat, a reminder that winter was drawing near. Beneath her paws she felt the roughness of stony patches, the velvety softness of dark green moss, the sponginess of damp soil giving way beneath her formidable weight.

But it was her sense of smell that was most acute. She sniffed the air, picking up the subtlest of scents: the decaying leaves, still lying in damp clumps along the rocky forest floor; the dank soil, rich and dense; the pungent needles of the evergreens, dry and brittle as they lay scattered on the ground.

There were other smells, as well. Animal smells. Rabbits and squirrels, birds in their nests for the night, owls perched on the branches of trees . . . Never for a moment did the wolf forget that, tonight, as she traversed the forest, she was on a hunt.

Suddenly she came to an abrupt halt. She had picked up a scent that was more intriguing than most. Every muscle in the animal's strong, vigorous body tensed. Her heart pounded. Adrenaline rushed through her body with the intensity of an electric current.

Her sense of hearing was keen. A few hundred yards away, she could hear the rustling of dried leaves. Her familiarity with the forest was so great she knew precisely where she would find her prey. Without another moment's hesitation, the wolf broke into a run.

Zeroing in on her prey was exhilarating. Never did she feel more powerful than when she experienced her own strength at its height. She was invigorated by the knowledge that she was in control—that of all the animals who roamed the forest during the night, she was the reigning queen.

Yet through it all, even as she relished the most subtle of sensations, one thought continued to echo through the wolf's mind.

You have crossed the line. You have made the choice to shapeshift. You have consciously decided to become the most hated thing you have ever known.

And then the one word echoed through her head; the word capable of causing her to tremble inside, two simple syllables that elicited in her a feeling of such absolute horror that it gripped her heart like an iron clamp.

Werewolf.

She knew what she was. Despite the urge to succumb to her bestial instincts, to lose herself entirely in her animal strength, she could not forget she was a human who had shapeshifted into animal form.

She could not run away from the reality: she had been unable to resist the lure of changing into a werewolf.

Despite the thrill, despite the exhilaration that transported her to a feeling of power, of joy greater than any other she had ever experienced, she could not forget that she was not an animal at all, but a seventeen-year-old girl, seduced by a supernatural force so horrific and strong that it was capable of enticing her away from the people she loved, the values she held dear, every aspect of her life that she treasured. . . .

She pushed herself onward, running even

harder than before, determined to carry through on the choice she had made.

Prepared to kill.

When she was less than fifty feet away, the giant beast slowed to a halt, her surefooted paws sinking into the soft soil at the edge of a small clearing. Silently she watched the deer, waiting for the right moment.

And then, in an instant, her prey was forgotten. Something new had come into the forest. Something heavy . . . oppressive . . . *evil*.

Its presence was so strong it was palpable. She could feel it in the air, as thick as the mist rising off the sea, as dense as the fog that blanketed the tall, dignified cedars in its mysterious white cloak. She could smell its putrid odor, her sensitive nostrils stinging from its pungency.

But her reaction was more than physical. Her awareness of this new presence that had come into the forest elicited a feeling so dark that it struck deep within her heart. It encroached upon every part of her body.

It penetrated her very soul.

That feeling had a name: *terror*.

And then, there in the forest, she heard the terrible rumbling sound. The entire earth seemed to tremble. The evil presence surrounded her, so solid it was smothering.

And then she saw them. Three horses, as black as the night. They were huge, standing much taller than any ordinary horses. Their massive chests heaved, rising and falling rhythmically. Impatiently they stamped the ground with their powerful hooves, their tremendous nostrils flaring.

Yet it was not the horses themselves that caused the fear to rise up inside her. It was the three horsemen who sat astride them. The men sat without moving, without showing any signs of life. Their shoulders were broad, their stature impressive. They were swathed in dark cloaks, the great folds of fabric tumbling down around them. Loose-fitting hoods concealed their faces.

She had seen them before. She had been alone that other time, as well, traveling through the forest in the dead of night.

When they approached her, her first instinct had been to recoil in fear. Yet despite her knowledge that they embodied evil, that they were seeking something she should not give, she had been drawn to them. . . .

Tonight, shapeshifted into the form of a wolf, she once again stood before them. She felt the fear. She knew they were evil.

She understood that she was their prey, in the same way the lone deer had been the prey of the mighty wolf.

Run! a voice deep inside her commanded. *Get away while you can!*

Yet again she was compelled to stay.

And then the horseman in the middle spoke, his voice tinged with an iciness that cut through her like the razor-sharp blade of a knife.

"You . . . are . . . ours."

The horseman pronounced each of the words slowly, rolling the three simple syllables around in his mouth as if he were savoring each one.

The wolf's mind clouded. She raised her head, her ears pricked as the words resonated through her head. Desperately she tried to make sense of them.

And then she understood.

She recoiled, her ears flattened, her shoulders hunched, her head lowered in a position of fear.

Forgetting for a moment that she was a wolf, Miranda opened her mouth to scream. Closing her eyes, she threw back her head.

The sound that escaped was a howl, so mournful and so filled with despair that the birds nesting in the branches of the trees took flight.

And then a new thought formed in her mind.

I am theirs.

The thought was more terrifying than the horsemen themselves. The meaning of what she'd done struck her with horrifying force.

Miranda began to tremble. She knew now what she was. The evil presence had triumphed. She had surrendered to it. She *was* theirs. Everything she despised, everything she had fought against . . . everything she had struggled to banish from the life of Garth Gautier, the person she loved most in the world.

She lay down on the forest floor, defeated. She could no longer deny the truth—even when that truth tore through her like the jagged edge of a weapon, inflicting upon her a pain so brutal she experienced it in body, mind, and soul.

And then, suddenly and without warning, the feeling began to fade. A tremendous weight was being lifted from her shoulders. Someone, something, was easing the pain, freeing her from the agony twisting inside. Surprised, her eyes flew open.

The horsemen were gone.

In their place there was a light. It was so pale that at first she thought it was simply the moonbeams, reflecting off the mist rising through the forest, glinting off the few dew-covered leaves that still clung hopefully to the trees.

Yet the light emitted a warmth, a welcome heat that slowly enveloped her. It offered comfort, refuge, and above all, hope. . . .

Miranda could feel the fear slipping away. In its place, a sense of peace washed over her. Her muscles relaxed, her heartbeat slowed. As she basked in the light, she slipped into a state of serenity.

How good it felt! The light . . . the warmth . . . so welcome, so peaceful . . .

Yet something was troubling her. In the back of her mind, still muddled by all that was happening, was a sense of confusion. Of puzzlement. The question of why, of who, of *what*, tugged at her.

Before long she remembered.

She had felt this presence before.

The words of Featherwoman, the wise old Native American woman who lived on the edge of town, came back to her, playing through her mind as loudly and as clearly as if she were hearing them for the first time.

"You are not alone, Miranda. You must never forget that. The good narnauks . . . they are on your side."

Miranda understood then that the good narnauks, the virtuous spirits who lived in the forest, had protected her. They were strong, she knew, their goodness as powerful as the evil embodied by the three horsemen.

Suddenly the urge to luxuriate in the power that came from shapeshifting was gone. No longer did she long to race beneath the black winter sky, no more did she crave the hunt.

Now she yearned to be one with the light.

Already she could feel herself changing back. Slowly the elongated jaw of the wolf shrank back to the size of a human's. She watched, marveling, as the lustrous coat of dark hair, glinting with strands of red, gave way to the smooth skin of a young woman. The powerful limbs reshaped, becoming sturdy legs and slender, graceful arms. . . .

Stumbling toward a grassy knoll at the edge of the forest, Miranda fell into an exhausted heap. Her chest heaved as her breaths came in gasps. She struggled to quiet her pounding heart, her eyes closed as she lay with her head cushioned by the soft green tufts.

So many feelings washed over her. Relief that she had escaped the evil power, eluded the three horsemen. Satisfaction that she had chosen to abandon shapeshifting, resisting its lure. Regret, as well, as the sweet memory of the freedom of running through the forest, wild and free, began to fade.

And then she sensed that she was not alone. Fear gripped her once again, and she opened her eyes, already on guard against what she might encounter.

She found herself gazing into a pair of blue eyes. She recognized them instantly. In them she saw concern. Affection. Compassion.

And then it rushed over her, nearly overwhelming her with its intensity: *love.*

Garth stood in the middle of the ballroom, his hands clasping Miranda's shoulders. He could not bring himself to look into her face.

Instead, Garth stared past her. He took in the beauty of Cedar Crest, the mansion in which he lived—the palatial estate that for generations had belonged to the Gautier family. The house consisted of more than thirty rooms, all of them decorated in the style of a French country manor, each one more ornate than the last.

The ballroom was the jewel of the house. Every inch of the cavernous space was elegant: its dark green marble floor, the intricate hand-carved frieze running along the edge of the high ceiling, the elaborate cornices gracing the top of each window.

One long wall was lined with mirrors. The wall directly opposite consisted almost solely of glass panes, French doors that led outdoors to the garden. White curtains covered them, their fabric sheer and so fine it billowed with the slightest movement of air.

Yes, the house was magnificent. But already Garth could see the subtle changes. Only a few weeks earlier, Cedar Crest had been transformed by Miranda's love, a love so powerful it had restored the decaying mansion, neglected for decades, to the magnificent showplace it had originally been.

Yet as he looked around, he could see that along with Miranda's fall came the beginnings of Cedar Crest's demise.

Already the shiny gilt trim was beginning to flake. The luster was gone from the wood on the ornamental cornices. Through the open doorway, leading to the rest of the house, he could see that the hand-painted murals in the hallway outside had also changed. The faces of the figures on them—plump, pink-cheeked cherubs, lovers gazing at one another fondly, clusters of animals coexisting in peace—had lost their radiance. Now there was a terrible sadness in their eyes.

Garth, too, felt a terrible sadness.

And then he looked into Miranda's eyes. His heart tightened when he saw that she, too, was showing signs of her fall. Yes, she was still beautiful. But there was a wildness about her that frightened him. Her thick mane of dark wavy hair, framing her face like a halo, was disheveled, with dried leaves and small bits of twigs tangled in it. Her skin, usually creamy with subtle peach tones, was uncharacteristically pale—the same pale shade as the full moon on a wintry night. Her forehead was furrowed, her full mouth tense, her expression drawn.

What haunted him most was the look in her eyes.

He had always lost himself in Miranda's eyes. They were dark, a rich brown color that reminded him of the earth after the rain. Through them, he could usually see into her soul. He had seen lightness there, and purity, and love.

Now, as he looked into them searchingly, he saw a turbulence that made his blood run cold.

She is lost to me.

Oh, Miranda! he thought, despair welling up inside him with such force it was almost a physical pain. My poor, sweet Miranda! It is happening. The one thing from which I vowed I would protect you. The horror that I've known all along . . . that I've known in my heart could only be worse if it became part of you. The horrific fate that from the start I've wanted to save you from—so much so that at first I resisted the urge even to speak to you.

They have seduced you.

He knew it was true; the dull ache in his heart told him so. She had tasted the freedom, the glory, the magnificent power that was part of shapeshifting. And she had found it so enticing that she had chosen to disregard the price.

Standing there, grasping her shoulders, seeing her transformed into this being that chilled his very soul, Garth thought back to the first time he'd seen her. It was in October, when autumn had just begun spreading its rainbow of rich reds, oranges, and yellows over the Oregon coast. Miranda had been standing in the schoolyard with two of her girlfriends.

They had hurt her, their words pummeling her like stones. And as he had watched, he'd felt her sorrow as if it were his own.

Yet he'd sensed her strength. It had pulled him toward her, elicited feelings deeper than any he had ever known before. He wanted to protect her, to make it all right.

Immediately he had reached out to her with

his heart and his soul. He had seen in her a beauty, an innocence, that he had never seen before, not in anyone.

Garth had known, even then, that there was a special connection between them. He'd sensed that being together was their destiny.

That thought had filled him with terror.

He blinked, anxious to forget that moment, instead wanting to concentrate on the here and now. And then another thought came to him: *maybe it hadn't been her choice to shapeshift.* Perhaps once again the evil power had overcome her resistance, overpowered her in a struggle no mortal soul was strong enough to win.

Please, please, he thought. *Don't let it have been her choice. Make it have been the doing of the evil power, something far beyond her control. . . .*

"Miranda." His voice was thick. "I must know. Why did you shapeshift again? What made you do it? Was it the evil power? Did it overwhelm you . . . ?"

Even before she spoke, Garth knew what her answer would be. He could see it in her eyes, in the way they clouded over. And in the way she looked down, no longer able to meet his gaze.

"I—I didn't mean for it to happen. I know it's dangerous. I know it's wrong. . . ." Her voice trailed off. She bit her lip, remaining silent for what seemed an eternity. And then, grabbing his shoulders, she looked into his eyes beseechingly.

"Oh, Garth! I couldn't stop thinking about it! Whatever I did, whoever I talked to, it was always there. A yearning, a longing, a—a craving I couldn't forget. That wonderful feeling, Garth! The exhilaration! Surely you know what I'm talking about. Once you've experienced it, how can you ever willingly give it up?"

He stood stiffly, unable to believe what he was hearing. Yet the look on her face told him it was true. She looked more animated, more alive, than he'd ever seen her. And the wildness in her eyes: it was still there, illuminating their darkness like the flames of a fire burning out of control.

And then one single syllable emerged from his lips: "*No!*"

Her face crumpled. "Oh, Garth! I'm sorry! I know it's terrible. But I couldn't resist. I understood that it was a mistake, I understood that it was dangerous . . . but I didn't care. I lost control. I—I . . ."

She collapsed against him, burying her face in his shoulder. Great sobs racked her body, erupting from deep within.

Garth could feel the hardness inside him melting. He held her tightly, clasping her against him, feeling her despair.

"My poor Miranda! I know, I know. You're frightened. But we'll fight this. We'll fight it together. Somehow, we'll find a way out. . . ."

"I—I saw them again." Slowly Miranda pulled

away from Garth. When she raised her head, her cheeks were streaked with tears.

"Who?"

"The three horsemen." She swallowed hard. "In the forest." Miranda was silent for a long time before she said, "He spoke to me, Garth."

"'He?'"

"The horseman in the center."

"Tell me. What did he say?"

"He said, 'You . . . are . . . ours.'"

A jolt ran through Garth's body, as if an electric current had been shot through every one of his nerves.

The girl leaning against him suddenly seemed like a stranger. Someone distant . . . someone dangerous. Instead of love, he felt repugnance.

When she spoke, the softness of her voice surprised him. "Hold me, Garth. I'm so afraid."

And then the aversion he had felt for that fraction of a second passed. He saw her for what she really was. A young woman who was caught in a trap. A girl who, like him, was vulnerable to forces so great and so powerful that she could not hope to fend them off by herself.

A girl who, except for him, was completely alone.

"Don't be afraid, Miranda." Garth's voice was tender. He reached up and gently stroked her cheek. "Remember: no matter what happens, we have each other."

"We have more than each other."

He frowned.

"After I saw the three horsemen," she told him, "I felt another presence. The good narnauks. They led me back, Garth. They helped me change into human form . . . to leave the beast behind."

Garth thought back to the words of Featherwoman. In their quest for an end to the terrible curse that had plagued Garth Gautier ever since he was fifteen years old—the curse that transformed him into a werewolf every twenty-nine days under the pale light of the full moon—he and Miranda had sought the advice of the wise old Native American woman.

She had explained to Miranda that the narnauks were the spirits who lived all around, as much a part of nature as the forests. They were in the rocks and in the trees, in the sun and in the moon, in the animals. They could be heard in the whistling of the wind, in the bubbling of the stream, in the rustling of the leaves.

Garth knew there were good narnauks, positive, life-giving spirits . . . but there were bad narnauks, as well. They were evil beings, capable of terrible destruction, thriving on horrific deeds.

Their power, he knew, came from the most evil being of all.

"Yes," he said. "We have the power of good

behind us. We can triumph over the evil," Garth insisted. "Already we have learned so much about my family's curse . . . and about the force behind it. We will get through this, Miranda. I know we will."

Wrapping his arms around her protectively, gently pressing her face against his heart, Garth only wished he believed his own words.

CHAPTER
2

The cacophonous sounds of Overlook High School first thing on a Monday morning assaulted Miranda as she made her way through the crowded hallways. The harsh slamming of metal locker doors, students calling loudly to their friends, the relentless din of a never-ending stream of people shuffling across the hall. She longed to clamp her hands over her ears, to block it all out.

Her eyes were similarly sensitive. The lights seemed so bright. She squinted as she walked, trying to dull the flashing colors of the students' clothing, the bulletin boards dotted with art-work, the different shades of the walls and doors, usually calming but today overstimulating.

She walked slowly, her books clutched closely against her chest, her eyes fixed straight ahead. It took all her concentration just to get herself through the building, crossing the short distance from the side door near the bicycle rack to her locker.

It had been more than forty-eight hours since her transformation back from a werewolf, yet her senses were still unnaturally acute. She felt so different, so attuned to everything around her . . . but still, somehow, not a part of any of it.

She had expected the episode to be over. She had shapeshifted . . . then been saved by the good narnauks. Their positive, life-giving powers had reined her back in, even in the face of the three dark horsemen. And she'd been grateful, recognizing the danger of what she had done, anxious to put it all behind her.

But it hadn't been long before the yearning came back.

As soon as she'd left Cedar Crest early Saturday morning, the longing had returned. She'd begun to crave the feeling of running freely through the forest. To bask in the light of the new moon. To luxuriate in the power that came with shapeshifting into animal form. The strength. The ability to hunt down even the quickest, cleverest, most elusive prey.

Her body had twitched, her muscles missing the feeling of pushing themselves to their limit. A tingling sensation kept electrifying her skin, as if the absence of fur left her feeling vulnerable. She felt confined by being indoors. Weakness would suddenly come over her, making her so dizzy she had to grab onto a chair or door-frame to keep her knees from buckling.

She had given in to the urge to be outdoors. All day Saturday, Miranda had walked in the woods, replaying familiar scenes in her mind, again and again. She closed her eyes, unable to focus on the present as she gave in to the desire to be part of the forest in the way she had the night before. How she wished she could once again feel the wind, run unfettered, marveling at her own strength, her own power. . . .

By comparison, the civilized world was gar-ish. Harsh. Unfamiliar, even. Miranda felt disori-ented as she finally found her locker. It was a struggle, turning the combination, concentrat-ing as she struggled to remember the three numbers she knew would open its door. She leaned forward, blinking hard as she studied the dial, hoping to recall what at the moment seemed impossible.

"Miranda! *There* you are!" Elinor Clay was suddenly at her side. She was smiling broadly, her hazel eyes shining as she pushed back her light-brown hair.

She was one of Miranda's newest friends, yet she'd quickly become one of her closest. In fact, one of the difficulties of living with Garth's se-cret, Miranda had discovered early on, was hav-ing to keep it from Elinor. It had driven a wedge between them. It was smoothed over, at least on the surface, but it continued to haunt her.

Today, however, Miranda was so distracted that even her concerns about her friendship with Elinor felt far away.

"I was hoping we'd get together this weekend," Elinor went on. "I stopped by, but your mother said you were out walking in the woods."

"Yes," Miranda said distractedly. "I've been spending a lot of time there."

"I, on the other hand, spent most of the weekend studying. My English teacher just assigned a huge research project." With a sigh, Elinor added, "Since you got an A on that term paper you wrote on *Romeo and Juliet*, maybe you could give me a few pointers."

"Sure." Somehow Miranda had managed to open her locker. She stared at the contents, trying to make sense of what she was seeing. The stacks of textbooks and spiral notebooks and other school paraphernalia left her feeling overwhelmed.

"Great. How about this weekend?"

"This weekend?" Miranda turned, really looking at her for the first time since she'd appeared at her locker. She saw that Elinor looked confused.

"What's up, Miranda? Do you already have plans for the weekend?"

"I . . . it's just that . . . "

Suddenly Miranda could no longer force herself to make conversation, even with a girl she considered one of her closest friends. She grabbed an armload of books without checking to see which ones they were and slammed her locker door. "I'm not feeling very well, Elinor. I'll call you, okay?"

She dashed off, leaving Elinor behind. Miranda shut her eyes, trying to block out the sight of the hurt, bewildered expression on her friend's face.

She was plagued by it only for a few moments. Before long, even the regret she'd initially felt over having caused her friend pain faded. Instead she found herself remembering the joyous feeling of flexing her powerful muscles as she leaped over a creek, the rapture that accompanied inhaling the rich smell of the damp earth. . . .

She was so absorbed in her daydream that she didn't pay any attention to where she was going. All of a sudden she bumped into someone. Glancing up, she found herself face to face with Selina Lamont.

"Hello, Miranda!" she greeted her enthusiastically.

Selina, known around school for her outlandish taste in clothes, was living up to her reputation today. She was wearing a hot-pink shirt with a pair of purple stretch pants. Usually Miranda admired her boldness. Today she squinted to protect her eyes from the garish colors.

"Have you heard the latest?" Selina's large green eyes were open wide. "The whole school's buzzing about it."

Miranda shook her head to show she had no idea what Selina was talking about. And then a frightening thought entered her head. Was it possible Selina had heard something about *her*? Had word gotten out that Miranda Campbell had taken to changing into a werewolf, that she'd been seduced by the dark power capable of turning humans into wild beasts . . . ?

"It's Amy and Bobby." Selina was wearing a smug smile. "They broke up."

"Oh."

"'Oh?'" Selina looked astonished. "Is *that* all you have to say?"

"It's really not any of my business. . . ."

Impatiently Selina tossed her head. "Earth to Miranda! Have you forgotten that you and Bobby McCann were going out for *years* before Amy Patterson came along? Don't you care that your ex-boyfriend, the first major love of your life, has finally seen the light about what that girl is really all about?

"*And,*" she went on, dropping her voice to a conspiratorial tone, "haven't you figured out that this break-up means the captain of Overlook High's basketball team is *available* once again?"

Miranda stared at her for a long time before answering. "Selina," she finally said, striving to keep her tone calm, "I'm not interested in Bobby anymore. We're friends, of course, but that's it."

"Oh, right. Garth."

An uncomfortable silence hovered between them, Miranda remembering how Selina had been harsh in her judgment of Garth, ever since Miranda had first met him. Selina and Corinne had gleefully informed her that nasty rumors were circulating around school, rumors that Garth Gautier, the new boy in Overlook, was responsible for the surge of violence suddenly plaguing the sleepy little coastal town.

Miranda had been startled by this vicious side of Selina, one she'd never seen before. But she'd thought all that was behind them. Now she realized Selina still distrusted Garth. And that she may even have been holding Miranda's involvement with him against her.

"Why did Bobby and Amy break up?" she asked, trying to sound interested.

Selina frowned. "I'm still working on that. All I know is, Saturday night they went to a party together—and then went home separately. I heard that from Merrill. And Jackie told me *she* heard that Amy called Caroline first thing the next morning, and that she was in *tears*. . . ."

Suddenly Miranda lost patience. "This is all fascinating, Selina, but I really have to get to class."

For the second time in less than five minutes, Miranda dashed off, leaving a disappointed friend behind. Once again, she expected to feel regretful.

Yet that same disconnected feeling plagued her. It was difficult for her to believe she had once been satisfied with this life—a life of seeing her friends, going to school, keeping busy with hobbies that now seemed pointless. Even her desire to be on the stage, a part of a theater troupe, no longer held the same allure. The fact that she'd recently joined the Limelight Theater Company in Portland for the run of an experimental French play, her first foray into the world of professional acting, did little to excite her.

Now, she was convinced, she'd experienced something far greater. Making her way through the corridors, which were finally emptying out as students disappeared into the classrooms on either side, Miranda once again gave into the urge to replay in her mind the familiar scenes from her nocturnal run.

Miranda shook her head hard, turning into a classroom just as the bell rang.

Letting herself into the house late that afternoon, right after school, Miranda was startled to find her mother caught up in a whirlwind of activity.

"I'm upstairs!" Mrs. Campbell called gaily. "Come on up!"

Her voice sounded muffled. Curious, Miranda

dropped her schoolbooks onto the dining-room table and climbed the stairs up to the second floor.

She found her standing in the hallway on a stepladder, her head poked up into the attic crawl space on the other side of the trapdoor. Piled up on the floor all around her were boxes, half a dozen dusty cardboard cartons sealed with packing tape.

"Can I help you with those?" Miranda offered.

"Thanks, but I'm almost done." When Mrs. Campbell bent down so that her face finally appeared, her cheeks were flushed and her eyes were shining. In her hands, wrapped in clear plastic, was a wreath, just one of the many well-loved Christmas decorations that had been part of the family's holiday celebrations for as long as Miranda could remember.

"Christmas? Already?"

"Haven't you checked the calendar lately?"

Miranda realized she had been caught up in so many other things that she'd barely noticed that time of year was upon them again.

Mrs. Campbell handed her the wreath, then climbed down the ladder. "It's just a few weeks away. And I really want to make Christmas special this year."

She cast her daughter a meaningful look. Miranda simply nodded. She could imagine how her mother must be feeling. This, after all, was the first Christmas that all three Campbells wouldn't be celebrating the holidays as a family.

The past two months, since her parents had separated, had been trying. More than anything she'd wanted her parents to find their way back to each other . . . for the three Campbells to return to the way they'd been living before.

Lately she'd been heartened. Her parents had come to the Pacific Players' opening night performance of *Saint Joan* together. Afterward, her mother had reported shyly, they'd gone out for coffee and really talked to each other. They'd seen each other a few more times since then, but a cloud of uncertainty still hovered in the air. Still, Miranda never lost hope.

Now she realized that getting through the holiday season while things felt so unsettled was going to be difficult. She went over to her mother and hugged her.

"I'm covered with dust," her mother warned, laughing as she hugged her back.

"I don't mind. A little dust never hurt anybody."

"Maybe not. But poking around in a nasty old attic all afternoon is exhausting. How about a cup of tea?"

"Sounds perfect."

A few minutes later, Miranda and her mother were settled in at the kitchen table, a pot of tea and a freshly opened box of butter cookies between them. The atmosphere in the kitchen was warm and homey. Even so, as she sipped her hot tea, she found herself glancing through the window. Outside, the day was darkening, the sun fading to a pale yellow-white and the gray sky cold and uninviting. A chill came over her, and she shuddered. An ominous air hung over the earth . . . yet instead of feeling repelled, she was drawn to it. She longed to be outdoors. . . .

"How's school going?" Mrs. Campbell asked congenially. "You haven't said much about it lately."

"Sorry," Miranda said guiltily. "I guess I've just been . . . busy." Once again her gaze drifted to the kitchen window.

She started at the clinking sound of her mother's teacup hitting against the saucer.

"Miranda." The expression on her mother's face matched her somber tone. "I think you and I have to talk."

Instantly Miranda tensed. "What is it, Mom?" She tried to keep her voice light.

"I haven't said anything about this, mainly because I've been so wrapped up in everything that's been going on between your father and me. But, well, you haven't been yourself lately."

"I've been busy with so many things, Mom. School, the play, the audition with the Limelight . . ."

"I know that, honey. I know you've taken on

a lot. But it's more than that." Mrs. Campbell hesitated, meanwhile dabbing at a few cookie crumbs that had fallen onto the table. "You seem so distracted lately. As if you're off in another world. Maybe it's natural that you and I grow further and further apart, now that you're seventeen, but I can't help feeling you're hiding something from me."

Miranda was tempted to protest. Instead, she remained silent, keeping her eyes fixed on the rim of her teacup.

"Then there's all the time you've been spending away from home, and the late hours you've been keeping. I know you're head over heels in love with Garth, but . . ."

Mrs. Campbell smiled gently. "I don't want to sound like I'm prying, Miranda. You're nearly a grown woman, after all. And I've always trusted you. But I want you to know that if there ever *were* anything wrong, if you ever wanted somebody to talk to . . ."

"Thanks, Mom." Miranda reached across the kitchen table, taking her mother's hand in her own. "I'm fine, really. And everything is okay. I promise."

Her mother's expression remained serious for a few more moments. But suddenly the tension left her face. Smiling, she said, "You know what would be fun? A holiday party." With a shrug, she added, "I think spending the afternoon with all those decorations inspired me. But how about it? Would you like to have some friends over? We could decorate every inch of this house and bake ourselves silly. . . ."

Miranda could see that her mother was trying to do something nice for her, to come up with a special project they could do together. Yet while she recognized that her mother's intentions were good, Miranda had no desire to undertake such a venture.

She was trying to think of a polite way to decline when a wave of guilt washed over Miranda. Her mother had had a difficult time lately. Her own reservations aside, she wanted to be supportive.

"I think it's a great idea, Mom."

"Oh, good! Now, let's see . . . I wonder if I still have that red tablecloth that belonged to my mother. It would be perfect on the dining-room table. And if you and I put our heads together, we could probably come up with a wonderful centerpiece. Something with evergreens and pinecones, maybe some red ribbons . . ."

"Maybe we'd better get out the calendar," Miranda said. Much to her own surprise, she was already getting caught up in her mother's excitement. "It sounds as if you've already got this whole thing planned. As soon as we pick a date, I can start calling people and inviting them."

"How about the weekend after this next

one?" her mother suggested, pointing to the calendar Miranda had taken down from the bulletin board hanging on the kitchen wall. "It's still early in the month, but that should mean your friends' schedules won't be filled with family commitments yet."

"Sounds great." Miranda leaned over and gave her mother a quick hug. "What a fantastic idea, Mom. Now, before I go crazy calling everybody I know, how many people do you think I should invite?"

When the telephone on the wall rang, the two of them burst out laughing.

"See that? Word has already spread!" Miranda was still laughing as she answered. "Hello?"

"Hello, Miranda."

Her smile faded as she recognized the voice on the other end of the line. It was Corinne's mother.

"Mrs. Davis! What a surprise. Is everything all right?"

"Everything is wonderful," the woman replied, the joyful tone of her voice complementing her words. "Corinne has just come out of her catatonia."

Mrs. Davis hesitated before adding, "She's asking for you, Miranda. Will you come?"

CHAPTER
3

Miranda was nervous as she stood in the doorway of Corinne's bedroom. The last time she'd been here, just a few weeks earlier, the blinds had been drawn and the room somber. She remembered that visit well. Corinne had sat in her bed, her unseeing eyes staring straight ahead, her arms wrapped tightly around a tattered teddy bear. The mere sight of her had been enough to tear Miranda's heart in two.

Yet as she knocked lightly on the open door, Miranda could already see today's visit would be different. This time, the blinds were pulled up to let in the pale December sunlight. A vase of brightly colored flowers was on the dresser. There were other items scattered there, as well: a brand-new scarf in bright colors, the price tag still attached; the latest issues of Corinne's favorite magazines; a package of imported cookies.

Miranda turned to Mrs. Davis and smiled, sharing the excitement she knew she must feel over her daughter's recovery.

Returning the smile, Mrs. Davis said, "I'll leave you two alone."

Corinne, sitting on the edge of the bed, looked pale and thin. The clothes she was wearing hung on her. Her long hair, a dark shade of blond highlighted with golden streaks, was pulled back into a ponytail. It was carefully brushed, yet had none of its usual luster. With her shoulders slumped and her head slightly bowed, she looked haggard.

But as Miranda came into the room and Corinne lifted her eyes, Miranda thought she saw a spark in them. She knew only too well that Corinne had gone through a difficult period. For weeks she'd been lost to the world, curled up inside herself as she called upon whatever inner resources it took to help the victim of a trauma recover. But the light in her eyes, however faint, gave Miranda hope for the first time since she'd retreated from the rest of the world.

"Corinne." Her first instinct was to run over and throw her arms around her. Yet she sensed she needed to proceed with caution. "You look great."

Corinne laughed hollowly. "You mean I look great considering the fact that I haven't left this room since October. I haven't left this *bed*."

Miranda swallowed hard. "What I mean is,

it's good to see you up and around again. And I'm so happy about the reports I'm hearing about how well you're doing."

"The doctors say I'm fine. Physically, anyway. And there have been a million doctors buzzing around me. My parents even got a specialist to come down here from Portland."

"They wanted so badly for you to get well."

Corinne barely seemed to have heard. "Want to see my scars?" she asked. Wrinkling her nose, she added, "They're really gross."

Without waiting for an answer, she pulled up her green sweater. Across her stomach was a huge welt, a red ridge that must have been eight inches long. On her side, just below her rib cage, were smaller marks, dark pink lines that were parallel to one another: the marks of an animal's claws. All the wounds were nearly healed, yet it was clear they would leave scars for a long time to come.

Miranda shuddered, quickly looking away. "I'm sure that, over time—"

"There are others, too. I'll show them to you sometime." With a shrug, Corinne added, "The scars aren't so bad. Just think: they'll give me something to show off in the locker room before gym."

"Oh, Corinne!" Suddenly all the emotion Miranda had been striving so hard to contain burst forth. "I'm so sorry this happened to you!"

Tears welled up in her eyes. She was one of

two people who knew what had actually happened that night, underneath the full moon. Garth had described the scene to her in detail.

He had been Corinne's attacker. The boy Miranda loved had inflicted those grotesque wounds, those long streaks of red that marred Corinne's youthful skin. It was he who had terrified her so badly that for weeks she had retreated deep inside herself, far away into a place in which no more pain or fear could touch her.

Garth . . . under the control of the horrific curse, the evil power that caused him to shapeshift.

"I feel for you, Corinne," Miranda said, her voice nearly a whisper. "And I've been so worried about you. We *all* have. Everyone at school has felt so bad."

Corinne lowered her eyes.

"Do—do you know what happened that night?" Hesitantly Miranda added, "It must have been so awful—" She stopped. "Or maybe you'd rather not talk about it."

Corinne was silent for a long time. She still kept her eyes fixed on the floor. And then, raising her head just enough that her gaze shifted to the dresser, she said, "I can't remember much. All I do remember is running toward the woods, so terrified I could hardly breathe. My heart was pounding. I ran and ran as fast as I could. But somehow I knew no matter how fast I went, it wouldn't be fast enough. . . . It was like a nightmare."

Miranda listened silently.

"It was an animal, you know. At least that's what the police told me. A woman came by yesterday—Officer Vale. She said it was probably the same one that attacked Andy Swensen. And a bear was mauled in the same way—"

"Maybe it's not a good idea to be thinking about it so much." Miranda's tone was pleading.

"There's more." Corinne paused. "I remember—I remember the feeling of it knocking me down. I can still feel its weight on me. The pain of its jaws closing around my arm—"

"Miranda." Mrs. Davis's harsh voice cut through the room. "Wouldn't you like something to drink? I'm sure you must be thirsty after helping Corinne catch up on all the school gossip she's missed while she's been out."

"Yes, Mrs. Davis," Miranda said, her tone apologetic. "That sounds great."

Miranda glanced at Corinne. Her eyes were cast downward, fixed on her hands, which were folded in her lap.

Tears stung Miranda's eyes as she cut across the Davises' lawn and headed for home. In part, they were tears of relief. Her long-time friend had been lost to her for so many weeks—longer, even, due to the animosity that had developed between them during *Saint Joan*—and now she was back. Now, at last, she was recovering from her trauma. She was doing so well, in fact, that her doctors had told her she'd be ready to return to school by the end of the week.

But the tears filling Miranda's eyes were also tears of remorse. She couldn't forget that Garth had been responsible for Corinne's terrible condition in the first place.

But it wasn't Garth! she reminded herself as she headed off the main road, down a quiet dirt path that ran along the forest. It was the beast who was responsible . . . the beast that the Gautier family curse still forced him to become. He'd never hurt anyone—not on his own. It was the cruel, merciless power that was so strong, no mortal had the capacity to resist it.

She swallowed hard, remembering too well her own experiences with that force, the way she'd relished her own dark strength.

That wasn't me! a voice inside her screamed. *It was the evil power. I was helpless in its presence, I was out of control. . . .*

And then another image burst into her mind. She remembered another time she had been out of control, once again a pawn in a game played by forces that existed on another plane, far beyond either her experience or her comprehension.

One night in November, when she and Garth were at Cedar Crest, they had been interrupted by two intruders. Miranda had been wrenched abruptly from the deep sleep she'd slipped into, lying in front of the fireplace in the parlor. Immediately she'd sensed danger. Yet even before she had a chance to react, she could feel herself being pulled outdoors. Invisible fingers grasped her wrists, tugging at her impatiently. Barely audible voices whispered in her ear: "Hurry! Hurry!"

The moment she'd stepped out of Cedar Crest, she had understood.

And then her thoughts, her actions, even her feelings ceased to be her own.

Miranda had fallen into a trance. She was aware of what was going on around her. She even knew the part she was playing in the scenario. Yet it was as if she were watching it all from a distance, a place far, far away . . . as if the person in Miranda Campbell's body was not really Miranda Campbell at all.

Standing in the doorway, she saw that the carriage house was aflame, and the fire was already spreading to the forest surrounding Cedar Crest. Cloaked in her hypnotic state, Miranda watched herself walk slowly across the grass, her bare feet crossing rough stones and sharp gravel without experiencing any feeling. On one side was the burning forest; on the other, the inferno that was the carriage house.

Yet she felt none of the heat of the raging fires. Instead, she was cool and refreshed. A wonderful sense of serenity came over her as she lifted her face toward the sky, meanwhile reaching upward.

In the end, she had triumphed. More accurately, the good spirits had instilled in her the power to overcome the evil intentions of another human being.

But the satisfaction she'd garnered from that victory proved short-lived. Miranda had quickly realized there was no reason to rejoice. Not when she and Garth still faced formidable odds . . . not only those with their roots in the supernatural world, but those right here among her peers, as well.

Miranda quickened her pace, more determined than ever to find a way to put an end to the horrific curse that tormented the man she loved—the curse that had ensnared her, as well.

She'd reached the edge of the woods. It was getting late; the grandfather clock in the Davises' living room had told her it was nearing five when she left. The daylight was nearly gone. Miranda reminded herself that the first day of winter, December twenty-first, was only three weeks away. No wonder a cloak of blackness had fallen over the sky. A few stars shone through weakly, their golden light pale glimmers that were nearly lost against the field of darkness.

The moon was on the rise, a gentle crescent. It would be a little more than three weeks before it was full. . . . The thought drifted lazily into Miranda's mind. It took a few seconds before she realized the moon would be full the night of the winter solstice. The shortest day of the year—the coldest, the most forbidding—would this year be illuminated by the eerie glow of the full moon.

Miranda shuddered, pulling her jacket more closely around her. She realized she'd stopped walking. Instead she hesitated at the edge of the forest. There were two routes home. The one through town was longer, but a much easier path to follow. The shortcut, meanwhile, took her through the woods.

The forest. Did she dare step inside? Or had all the events of the past weeks changed it into a place that was no longer safe?

Or perhaps the forest hadn't changed at all. Perhaps it was simply *she* who had changed.

She stood at the edge, peering inside. How beautiful it was! The magnificent cedars, towering evergreens reaching up toward the sky, their green branches sweeping the air with a grand gesture, their peaked tops cutting along the edge of the horizon. The gnarled deciduous trees, now bare of leaves, their dark arms undulating in the wintry wind. The lengthening shadows that crept over the forest floor, crisscrossing over the beds of silky green moss, the moist brown-black bogs filled with decaying leaves, the jagged gray rocks that looked like pieces of sculpture.

Yes, it was beautiful. And despite all that had happened, it continued to beckon to her.

Miranda could not resist.

She stepped into the forest. Immediately a feeling of peace descended upon her. She *belonged* here. She always had. This was a magical place, a wondrous place. Here, she could experience life in a way she could nowhere else. Here, she could experience *herself* in a way she could nowhere else.

She inhaled deeply, her lungs eagerly taking in the clean, fresh air as she walked. Her step was confident as she made her way across the variations in terrain.

And then, suddenly, she heard a noise. It sounded like the snapping of a twig.

Quickly she turned. She found herself looking directly into a pair of burning jet-black eyes.

"Evil!" a hoarse voice hissed.

Miranda froze. The condemnation in the voice of the woman standing before her, her face tensed into a grotesque scowl, was unmistakable.

She knew this woman well. The proud stance of the aged frame, hunched over and frail. The craggy features that remained strong, even though the brown skin was wrinkled, withered with age. Most of all, the wisdom that she emanated.

"Featherwoman!" Miranda gasped.

"They have you." Once again she spoke in a low, rasping voice. "Twice, Miranda. Twice you have chosen to shapeshift."

"I only wanted to learn about it!" she protested. Echoing in her own ears, her words sounded weak. Hollow. They were swallowed up by the vastness of the forest the moment she spoke them.

"No, Miranda. I know the truth." Featherwoman brought her face right up to Miranda's. She was so close Miranda could feel the old woman's breath against her cheek. "You must find the way, Miranda. The time is near. Prepare yourself for the fight!"

"What fight? Featherwoman, please tell me. I—I don't understand—"

"When the moon is full. When the winter is upon us. *Then* you must fight the final battle."

A chill ran down Miranda's spine. The words rang through her ears as Featherwoman turned, disappearing into the forest so quickly and so silently that Miranda wondered if the whole encounter had simply been something she'd imagined.

When the moon is full. When the winter is upon us.

She knew what that meant. Featherwoman had been talking about the winter solstice.

It was only three weeks away.

That was the night. That was when the final battle would be fought.

CHAPTER
4

When the moon is full. When the winter is upon us. Then you must fight the final battle.

Featherwoman's haunting words were still ringing through Miranda's head on Wednesday. The magnitude of what the old woman had said was almost too much for her to bear, so she threw herself into the holiday party she and her mother were planning.

She was finding it a relief, having something so simple to think about. It had actually been fun, sitting down with her mother to draw up a list of what they'd need. Immediately after school, Miranda threw her books into her bicycle basket and headed straight for Norton to do some shopping.

As she pedaled along the side of the two-lane highway, she tried to concentrate on the party. Yet her mind kept drifting. Instead of focusing on the cars passing by, she looked longingly toward the wooded areas beyond the farms flanking the road. She could hear things, sounds she'd never noticed before . . . or perhaps had never been capable of hearing before. The snapping of a small branch, the flapping of a bird's wings, the scampering of a squirrel's tiny feet as it hurried across a carpet of dried leaves.

Even from the road, a few hundred yards away from the edge of the forest, she could smell the rich, damp soil, the decaying logs, the scent of small animals. How she longed to be in the midst of the dense growth, running, hunting, experiencing the freedom. . . .

Miranda was relieved when the buildings of Norton came into view. Being so close to the forest was too tempting. If only she could keep away, she reasoned, perhaps then she would be able to resist.

The neighboring town, three miles inland, was much larger than Overlook. Coasting down Moss Avenue, the main street, Miranda glanced at the stores she'd grown so familiar with: a card shop, a clothing boutique, a gift emporium. Today she was not the least bit interested in browsing in them. She knew she would have to force herself to go inside. She had to, to keep from disappointing her mother.

Also on Moss Avenue was her father's veterinary office. She rode by slowly, wondering if she should stop off to pay him a visit. She generally did, whenever she made a trip into Norton. But she'd been so distracted lately. . . . Finally, deciding she saw her father all too rarely these days, she veered into his parking lot. She leaned her bicycle against the trim white building, right under the sign that read DR. BRYAN CAMPBELL, DOCTOR OF VETERINARY MEDICINE, and headed inside.

Just as she'd expected, she found her father sitting at his desk, sorting through some medical files. Glancing at the clock on the wall, she saw it was almost time for his evening office hours to begin.

"Hi, Dad!"

He glanced up, his face immediately registering surprise. "Miranda! How nice to see you."

Miranda surveyed his office, blinking in the harsh fluorescent light. It was a cheerful, cluttered place. Veterinary journals were stacked up haphazardly on the shelves that lined one wall, and the usual piles of paper and medical forms were strewn across his desk. "It looks as if you're as busy as usual."

Shaking his head slowly, Dr. Campbell said, "I keep telling myself it's a good thing I love what I do. Otherwise, I'd probably hate it."

Miranda laughed. She was glad she'd taken the time to stop. Just seeing her father was helping to make her feel like herself again. Already she could feel some of the tension that had had her so preoccupied dissipating. "I'm not staying long. I just stopped in to say hello."

Her smile faded and she became thoughtful. Something else had popped into her mind, not at all related to Garth but troubling nonetheless. "Dad," she said hesitantly.

"What is it, honey?"

"Ever since you moved out of the house back in October," she went on in the same hesitant tone, "I've been trying really hard to be optimistic. I know this is between you and Mom. And maybe I've been fooling myself, but I've been thinking all along there was a good chance this separation would turn out to be just temporary."

"Go on." Dr. Campbell's forehead was furrowed.

"But now it's getting close to the holidays." She took a deep breath, understanding that she had to go ahead and say what was on her mind. "And I've started to realize it won't seem like a real Christmas without you."

Instantly her father's expression softened. He came out from behind his desk and put his arms around her. "Oh, honey. I'm so sorry you've been worried. Your mother and I have already talked about this. And we decided that, if it's all right with you, we'd like to spend Christmas Day together, just the way we always have."

Miranda was so happpy she hardly knew how to respond.

"Did Mom tell you about the party?" she asked instead.

"Yes, and it sounds like a fine idea. Just the thing to kick off the season."

"Actually, it was Mom's idea. And it's all we've been able to talk about." Miranda was growing excited, and could almost believe for a moment that she was just a normal teenager. "In fact, I'm here in town to stock up on party supplies. Plates and cups and things for the table, some craft supplies so Mom and I can make a centerpiece—"

"And how do you propose to get all this home?"

"My bicycle basket is pretty roomy."

Her father looked surprised. "Sometimes I forget how self-sufficient you are, Miranda. You've been that way ever since you were a little girl. Always determined to do things by yourself, without help from anyone.

"Well, if you find your shopping spree makes handling your bike too tough, stop by on your way out of town. I'd be happy to give you a lift home."

Miranda resisted the temptation to ask her father if part of the appeal of taking her back to Overlook was that it would give him a chance to see her mother. Instead, she simply smiled.

"Did you get everything?" Mrs. Campbell

called from the living room as Miranda let herself in through the back door.

"I think so." She deposited two large bundles on the kitchen table.

"Goodness! It must have been some job, lugging all that home." Miranda's mother was standing in the doorway, her hands on her hips. "You should have stopped in at your father's. I'm sure he would have been happy to have piled all this in his Jeep along with your bike and brought you back here."

Miranda laughed. "Funny. That's exactly what he suggested when I stopped in at his office to say hello."

"And you didn't take him up on his offer?"

"No, I was fine on my bike." Miranda knew her mother well enough to see disappointment in her eyes.

As if to change the subject, Mrs. Campbell delved into the larger of the two bags. "Let me see what you bought." She had just come up with a package of pretty holiday plates when the telephone rang.

Miranda, who was closer to it, automatically reached out and picked it up. "Hello?" she said crisply.

"Hello, Miranda?"

"Jeff! How nice to hear from you!" Her tone had immediately become softer.

"So you know my voice already? I'm not

catching you at a bad time, am I?"

"No, I'm not busy."

Casting her a knowing smile, her mother slipped out of the kitchen.

"Well, Miranda, Saturday's the big day."

"The big day?" Miranda was confused by Jeff Jordan's indirectness. When she'd met the young actor during her audition for the Limelight Theater Company, she'd had the same reaction: uncertainty about whether she liked the charming, good-looking boy who seemed so sure of himself . . . or was put off by him.

She had to admit that he was excellent at what he did. The two of them had worked together at the audition, reading a scene from an experimental new play. Not only had she been impressed by his talent; she'd truly enjoyed interacting with him onstage. Yet she hadn't felt half as comfortable with his confident, almost arrogant manner when the words they were speaking to each other were not being read off the pages of a script.

"I'm talking about the big day we've all been waiting for," Jeff went on. "The first rehearsal of *La Rose* is scheduled to begin at ten A.M. *Sharp.* Of course, by David Singer's standards, that will probably mean ten thirty. Or maybe even eleven. Or I suppose it's possible that—"

"I'll be there at ten sharp," Miranda told him, laughing.

"Great. Then I'll make a point of being there at five minutes of ten. The cast members will be meeting onstage, although we'll probably just spend the morning sitting on uncomfortable folding chairs, giving the script a quick read-through. The really grueling rehearsal schedule won't start until after Christmas."

"Saturday at ten, then. Thanks for letting me know."

"So," Jeff went on in a casual tone, "how have you been?"

"Fine. Busy—"

"Not too busy, I hope." He hesitated. "What I mean is," he continued, his voice taking on a much softer tone, "I was wondering if you'd be able to stay in Portland Saturday evening. After the rehearsal, I mean. I'd like to show you some of the sights around town. Or if you prefer, we could go to a movie or have dinner. . . ."

Miranda's thoughts were racing. Was Jeff Jordan asking her out on a date? She was so surprised that it took her a few seconds to respond.

"Thank you, Jeff. It's nice of you to offer. But, well, I don't think I'll be able to. You see, I—"

She was about to explain that she was already seeing someone when he interrupted with, "Okay. I'll catch you next time.

"I'll be seeing you on Saturday, then," he went on. "And come prepared. At the audition, you saw David Singer playing the role of the pussycat.

But believe me, you haven't seen anything until you've seen David Singer starring as the lion!"

The face was menacing, with its cruel sneer exposing two even rows of teeth. The four gleaming fangs at the front of its mouth were sharp and nearly two inches long. Studying the head of the wolfskin he held in his arms, Garth attempted to view it objectively.

Instinctively he felt a wave of revulsion.

This monstrous beast, after all, was what fate dictated he himself become.

The wolfskin was indeed treacherous looking, with its fierce expression and enormous fangs. Yet at the same time he recognized that it possessed a beauty lacking in the creature he became upon shapeshifting.

It was more than mere size that differentiated the two beings, more than the fact that the werewolf's strength was so much greater than even the impressive power of the ordinary wolf. He had seen his own reflection in the waters of a stream, illuminated by the light of the full moon. There he had confronted the ugly snarl, the cruel glint in his eyes, the air of malevolence emitted by the beast into whose form he shapeshifted.

The wolf was just one of God's creatures, a part of the intricate food chain, killing for no other reason than to eat, to survive. The werewolf, however, had much more sinister origins and killed for sheer blood lust. The wolf was a beautiful animal—the werewolf was an uncontrollable beast.

Garth studied the artifact he had taken weeks earlier from the Overlook Public Library, sneaking downstairs into the basement museum after hours. He marveled over what had once been the skin of a magnificent animal. The hide was huge. The animal to which it had belonged had weighed more than a hundred and fifty pounds. When it stood on all fours, it was more than six feet long. Even Garth, with his well-developed muscles, had to strain to lift it.

Its thick fur, an almost luminescent shade of silvery gray with white flecks, was amazingly soft. Its snout was long and delicately pointed, its ears shaped like triangles, their sides gently curved.

Tonight, gazing at the wolfskin, illuminated by the moonlight shining through the windows of the drawing room at Cedar Crest, Garth could appreciate its beauty. But the beauty had been obscured by darkness. This ordinary wolfskin had become a tool of evil.

This wolfskin, after all, was what had enabled Miranda to change into a werewolf. And now that she had crossed the line, lived through the shapeshifting experience herself, she would never be able to go back. Never again would she be the same.

This wolfskin had stolen her innocence.

Now the evil power had her in its merciless grip.

Suddenly one of the French doors flew open, letting in a sharp gust of icy wind.

It can read my thoughts, Garth thought. *It knows how I feel . . . how I suffer.*

And it rejoices in my pain.

His resolve to free himself of the tyranny of the wolfskin—to prevent Miranda from ever again giving into the temptation to shapeshift— had never been stronger. Garth dragged the heavy wolfskin across the dark red marble floor of the drawing room.

He wanted only to protect her. To keep her from knowing what he knew . . . living the life he lived.

Even now, looking back on all that had happened to her so far, daring to anticipate what still might lie ahead, he knew he didn't possess the power to protect her.

No one did.

Yet he couldn't resist the urge to try. The wolf-skin grew heavier as he continued to drag it through the garden, toward the back of the property surrounding Cedar Crest, toward the forest.

As Garth got farther and farther away from the house, he noted with sadness the alarming rapidity with which it was once again becoming decrepit. Cedar Crest looked sorrowful, a black cloud hanging over it as if it were in mourning.

The windows were once again blank, unseeing eyes, the wooden shutters framing them drooped, the stones and bricks were chipped and pitted.

Shaking his head slowly, his heart aching with sadness and remorse, Garth climbed over a crumbled section of the wall surrounding the estate and headed into the forest, determined to carry out the one small attempt to undo what had already been done: to return the wolfskin to the place where it had originated.

The woods seemed particularly ominous tonight. The shadows were deep, the shushing made by the tall cedars swaying in the wind sounded like whispers no human being was meant to hear. The air was brisk, with a bite to it. Garth felt like an intruder, unexpected and unwelcome.

But he trudged onward, dragging the wolfskin over the rough terrain. He planned to bury it, to return it to the earth.

He wanted to find just the right spot.

And then he knew. He would bury it where Miranda had first shapeshifted into a werewolf, banishing it to the bowels of the earth in the same place where its dangerous powers had gripped her.

He continued on toward the clearing, not far from Cedar Crest yet very much a part of the forest. Standing there, the hide clutched in his arms, he found himself reliving the moment Miranda had first crossed over to the other side.

He remembered the moment she changed into a werewolf, and all that had accompanied her transformation: the ghoulish shadows that leaped out from behind trees, the low rhythmic rumble that sounded like drums resounding through the forest, the piercing shrieks that shot out of the dark, sounding like nothing of this earth.

Now, standing in that same spot, remembering, his heart ached. What had been set in motion, he feared would never be stopped.

With energy and determination, he dropped to his knees, digging in the moist ground. The dirt gave way easily. Digging a hole big enough to swallow up the wolfskin was not much of a challenge. In fifteen minutes, the task was complete.

Lowering the skin into the hole and then quickly covering it up with soil, Garth expected to feel a sense of relief. Perhaps even triumph. He waited, wondering if the good narnauks would rejoice . . . or the bad narnauks would rage. Yet he felt nothing.

As he walked away, his heart was as heavy as before. His despair, he realized, was rooted in the fact that, deep down, he knew his actions, his attempt at protecting Miranda from the curse, had been in vain.

CHAPTER
5

Jeff Jordan's unexpected invitation left Miranda with a peculiar feeling. She'd been so involved with Garth that it had never even occurred to her somebody else might ask her out—especially Jeff.

What she found even more disconcerting, however, was that she was actually flattered by his invitation. In spite of herself, Miranda's heart fluttered every time she thought of his telephone call. Compared to the boys she'd grown up with, Jeff seemed terribly sophisticated, not to mention one of the few people her age who shared her interest in the theater. Her cheeks grew warm every time she thought about the fact that she'd been noticed by someone like him.

Or maybe I simply misinterpreted what he said, she thought as she chained her bicycle to the metal rack outside Overlook High School the next morning. Perhaps he was just being friendly. I *am* the newest member of the theater company, after all. Maybe inviting me to spend Saturday evening with him was simply his way of trying to make me feel welcome.

That explanation was much easier to live with than the possibility that he had singled her out as someone he was interested in dating. Deciding she'd been too quick to read something into what was probably just an innocent suggestion, Miranda pushed the entire matter out of her mind.

Besides, she reminded herself as she hurried inside the school building, she had something much more pressing to think about. Today was Corinne's first day back at school.

Suspecting that Corinne might have some apprehensions about returning after an absence of more than a month, Miranda had made a point of telephoning her the night before.

"Tomorrow's the big day," she'd said enthusiastically. "Are you all set?"

"Actually, I'm a little nervous." Corinne's voice sounded weak. "It's not as if I were out because I had the flu. I keep imagining all the kids at school staring at me, whispering behind my back—"

"Most of the kids have just been worried," Miranda was quick to assure her. "Besides," she added encouragingly, "Selina and I will be there. Who's better at giving moral support than we are?"

Yet Miranda, too, was filled with apprehension

as she made her way toward her locker. There were bound to be questions. Rumors and speculations would undoubtedly be flying around the school. With Corinne's return, the whole incident would once again be fresh in everyone's mind. And she was fearful that sooner or later her own name would come up. Her name . . . and Garth's.

Selina and Corinne were waiting for her near her locker.

Next to Selina's characteristically bright outfit, Corinne looked colorless. Her face was still pale and gaunt. She was dressed in an outfit Miranda recognized as one of her favorites. But this morning the black pants with the beige shirt hung on her thin frame. Tied around her neck was the pretty scarf Miranda had noticed on her dresser, one of the many items Mrs. Davis had bought in celebration of her daughter's recovery. Even its cheerful colors did little to liven up her appearance.

"Welcome back!" Miranda greeted Corinne with a warm hug. "You look great."

"Doesn't she?" Selina said with forced enthusiasm. "I was just telling Corinne the exact same thing. Isn't it fabulous that she's back in school?"

"Yes. It certainly is," Miranda said happily.

"Thanks, you two." Corinne cast them both a grateful smile. "I just wish I was as convinced as everybody else seems to be that I'm really ready for this."

"You'll be fine," Selina insisted. "And everybody's going to be thrilled to see you again. You're going to be the center of attention all day.

"Come on. I'll walk you to our first-period class. You remember chemistry, don't you? Bunsen burners, test tubes . . . surprise quizzes?"

Corinne laughed. "Thanks, but I'm supposed to stop by the school nurse's office first thing." She shrugged. "Doctor's orders."

After she'd left, Selina grabbed Miranda's arm. "It's just as well Corinne's not around," she said, her voice lowered. "Let me walk you to English."

Puzzled, Miranda followed.

Selina waited until she and Miranda had walked down to the other end of the hall, out of earshot of the last few students rushing off to class. They stood outside Mr. Wexler's classroom, where Miranda had her first class of the day.

Selina leaned over, speaking in a loud whisper. "Okay, Miranda. Brace yourself. I've got the juiciest piece of news *imaginable*, but I didn't want to tell you in front of Corinne. Somehow, I don't think she's ready for this."

"Why not? What are you talking about?"

"You'll understand when I tell you."

Miranda wasn't in the mood for idle gossip. Glancing around, she noticed that the corridors were empty. "If I don't get inside that classroom in about thirty seconds, I'm going to be late."

"It'll be worth it. Miranda, I found out the most amazing thing." Selina's green eyes were narrowed. *"Werewolves!"*

Miranda froze. It took every ounce of self-control she possessed to keep from reacting.

"Werewolves?" she said, her voice surprisingly calm. "What on earth are you talking about?"

"That's the reason—"

"Miss Campbell," Mr. Wexler boomed, sticking his head out into the hallway. "Perhaps you've forgotten that school is a place for learning. I suggest you and your friend save your gossiping for the mall."

Miranda cast Selina a desperate look. "I'll talk to you later, all right?"

"It'll just have to wait until lunch." Selina was already halfway up the corridor, hurrying to her own first-period class.

Miranda's stomach was in knots as she took her seat in the front of the classroom. Was it possible that Selina had found out Garth's secret? she wondered, panic rising inside her. She couldn't imagine how. And if it turned out she really had, what would happen next? Would Selina go around telling everyone at school . . . and in town? Would anyone believe her? If they did, how would they react?

Mechanically she opened her spiral notebook and turned to a blank page. The blue lines on the page were nothing but blurs. Miranda had a feeling that sitting through the three hours of classes that still remained before lunch was going to be one of the most difficult things she had ever done.

"Now," she said, setting her lunch tray down next to Selina, "what's all this nonsense about werewolves?"

Selina turned to face her, her eyes already lit up with excitement. "It's the reason Bobby broke up with Amy!"

Instead of being relieved by her response, Miranda was simply confused. "I don't understand."

"Remember on Monday when I told you they broke up?"

Miranda nodded.

"I promised you I'd find out why, right? Well, I did." The expression on Selina's face was one of triumph. "And it has to do with werewolves!"

Miranda shook her head. In a guarded tone, she said, "I'm sorry, but I still don't get it."

"Okay." Selina took a deep breath. "It all began when Amy came up with this totally outrageous idea: that the creature that attacked both Andy Swensen and Corinne was a werewolf. Isn't that the craziest thing you've ever heard in your life?"

Miranda didn't know whether to breathe a sigh of relief . . . or be more concerned than ever. On the one hand, she was heartened by the fact that Selina was dismissing the whole idea as absurd. At the same time, Amy was still on the warpath. Not only was she determined to put herself in the center of all the controversy still gripping the town of Overlook; she was dangerously close to figuring out the truth.

"She's been watching too many late-night movies," Miranda said with a nervous laugh.

"Well, she doesn't *really* believe the attacker was a werewolf. Just that he *thinks* he is."

"What do you mean?"

Selina shrugged, meanwhile opening a diet soda. "Apparently Amy got hold of a book on—wait, let me get this right—lycanthropy." She pronounced the word slowly. "It's a term psychiatrists use to describe this really weird kind of mental illness. The person who's got this . . . this lycanthropy syndrome actually believes he turns into a wolf whenever the moon is full."

"I see." Miranda managed to keep her tone casual. "But what does all this have to do with Bobby?"

"What I heard is that when Amy started going around telling people this crazy new theory, Bobby got all bent out of shape. He told her she was completely nuts—not to mention a troublemaker and a busybody and a whole list of other things. From what I understand, they had a huge fight. The rest, as they say, is history."

"I'm not surprised that Bobby finally caught on to what kind of girl Amy is." Miranda was talking more to herself than to Selina.

Suddenly she remembered that for a while, Selina and Amy had been friends. She turned to Selina and in an apologetic voice said, "Not that she doesn't have her good side, too. I mean, you certainly thought so. The two of you were pretty good friends."

Selina made a face. "Bad judgment on my part. Look, Bobby and I both got roped in by Amy. It's as simple as that. She's a smooth talker, that one."

"Yes," Miranda agreed. "And I have a feeling she's not finished yet."

"Hey, here's Corinne!" Selina's face lit up. She pushed aside her schoolbooks to make room for their friend. "How's your first day back going?"

"I'm surviving," Corinne said with a little laugh as she set down her tray.

"I guess you've already realized you haven't been missing much. Especially after that ridiculous chem lab this morning. As if knowing how to titrate an acid is really going to improve my life!"

"Actually, it's kind of fun being back." Her movements slow and cautious, Corinne pulled out a chair. "I can't believe how much has happened while I was out. Just last period, I heard that Bobby and Amy broke up. I can't say I'm surprised—"

She stopped herself, casting a sheepish look at Miranda. "I'm sorry. Maybe I shouldn't be talking about this in front of you."

"It's all right. I'm not—"

"Well, well, well." Amy Patterson suddenly stood before them, her hands on her hips. She gave an arrogant toss of her head, sending a shimmer down her long cascade of pale blond hair. She was tall and slender, with a habit of laughing too loudly in a way that invariably made her the center of attention. Lately she'd begun wearing too much makeup, an effect that detracted from her natural prettiness, rather than highlighted it, and today was no exception. "Welcome back, Corinne."

"Thanks, Amy." Corinne barely glanced up.

Amy leaned forward, her eyes narrowing. "I heard you've still got horrible scars from your attack. Are they ever going to go away?"

Fury rose up inside Miranda. "Amy!" she cried. "I really don't think that's something Corinne feels like discussing—"

"It's all right," Corinne assured her. "I knew people would be curious. I've been expecting a lot of questions."

"I don't know about questions, but I think I might know some answers." Amy flicked her hair back over her shoulder. "About your mysterious attacker, I mean."

"Mysterious?" Corinne repeated. "I was attacked by a wolf. I still don't remember anything about that night, but there's enough evidence for a wolf attack to convince me. Miranda's father looked at my wounds and compared them to the ones that were found on Andy's body—"

"I know. They appeared to be the signs of an animal attack," said Amy. "Or so he *says*."

Corinne looked puzzled. "You don't believe him?"

"Let's just say I've been developing my own theory." Casting a meaningful glance in Miranda's direction, she added, "And whenever you're interested in discussing it, just let me know."

Miranda stood at her locker, still ruminating about the uncomfortable scene at lunch as she tried to concentrate on which books she would need for her next class. Amy's words stuck with her, echoing through her head. She suddenly presented a terrible threat, yet Miranda had yet to get a handle on how far she planned to go with it. Perhaps before long, she'd tire of her new "theory"—or else other people would tire of hearing about it. What she did know was that the short confrontation was eating away at her, making it difficult to concentrate on anything more demanding than getting through the day.

Still lost in thought, she gradually became aware that someone was standing uncomfortably close to her.

"Hello, Miranda."

Glancing to the side, she saw Dave Falco leaning against the row of lockers next to hers.

"Hello, Dave." She paused, unsure of whether to ask him the first question that came to mind. "How's Mark?"

"Not bad, considering. Second-degree burns are pretty serious, you know. His whole shirt was on fire. It's going to be weeks before he's back on his feet again."

The look in his dark brown eyes was intense. He leaned forward, putting his face right up next to hers. "I haven't forgotten what happened that night, Miranda. I'll never forget it as long as I live."

"I haven't forgotten, either," she returned crisply. "Nor have I forgotten the fact that you agreed you wouldn't say anything."

"Yeah, I know." Dave Falco hesitated, his steely gaze still unwavering. And then a cold smile crept slowly across his face. "But I never said I wouldn't *do* anything."

Later, Miranda opened her locker, prepared to stash her schoolbooks from the last few periods of the day, grab her jacket and whatever she needed for that night's homework, and get on her bicycle. She'd thought the day would never end, and now that it finally had, she could hardly wait to get away. And then something caught her eye. A piece of yellow paper, folded up several times, sat on her history textook, on the top shelf of her locker. Someone had pushed it through the vent.

Her heart began to pound, and she unfolded it quickly.

"I probably have no right to ask you this," she read, "but would you meet me after school today? I'll be at the Overlook Diner at three thirty."

At the bottom of the page, as if it had been an afterthought, was scrawled, "Please, Miranda. It's important to me."

It was signed, "Bobby."

"I'm really glad you came," Bobby said, plunging his hands deep inside the pockets of his jacket. "I wasn't sure if you'd show."

He was sitting opposite her at a corner booth at the Overlook Diner, a small place on the edge of town. It was all but deserted, affording them all the privacy they needed.

"Why wouldn't I?" Miranda's surprise was genuine.

Bobby glanced at her shyly. "You mean aside from the fact that I've behaved like a real jerk these last few weeks?"

Just then their waitress stopped by their table and placed a cup of hot chocolate in front of each of them. Before Miranda had a chance to express her surprise, Bobby said, "I hope you don't mind that I went ahead and ordered for you. I got here a few minutes early."

"Of course I don't mind."

"I haven't forgotten how much you like hot chocolate."

Miranda thought back to the first time she and Bobby had had hot chocolate together. It was their third date. They'd gone ice skating at a rink nearby, then stopped to take a break at the concession, sitting in a booth not unlike this one. They'd both laughed when Miranda leaned over to take a sip of her hot chocolate and got a drop of whipped cream on her nose. Bobby had leaned over and kissed it away.

There were so many moments like that. The first time they'd slow-danced together at the spring dance, during her freshman year, when she'd suddenly viewed her childhood pal in a whole different light. Their first kiss, outside on a summery night when the dark blue sky was covered with so many shimmering stars it looked as if it'd been sprinkled with fairy dust. The time he'd told her he loved her for the very first time, the two of them crunching through a carpet of bright orange and red autumn leaves.

There'd been bad moments, as well. Those had been concentrated at the end of their two and a half years together, when he began making it clear he was anxious for their relationship to advance to a more intimate level than she felt ready for.

"Anyhow," Bobby said, pretending to concentrate on stirring his hot chocolate, "I wasn't sure whether or not you were still talking to me."

"Of course I am," Miranda replied earnestly. "I've really missed your friendship, Bobby."

"Yeah. Me, too."

After a long, uncomfortable pause, Miranda said, "I heard about you and Amy." She tried to sound casual. "Selina told me."

"I'm sure she was only too happy to pass the word on," Bobby returned. "Along with everybody else at school."

"I think a lot of people were really surprised. I guess it seemed kind of . . . sudden. I did want to tell you that I'm sorry."

"I'm not." His tone was unexpectedly cold. "It really is for the best. I only wish—"

"What?"

"I wish I'd appreciated what I had before I went and threw it all away."

"With Amy?" Miranda asked, confused.

"With you."

She simply stared at him.

"Look, Miranda. I know I screwed up—big time. You and I really had something going there. And, well, I was too dumb to recognize that what we had was really . . ." He let his voice trail off.

"Special?" Miranda supplied the word in a

gentle tone.

"Yes. Special."

He hesitated for a moment, then reached over and took her hands in his. "Miranda, I know you're involved with that new guy. I've heard around school that the two of you are really tight. But if I thought there was even a chance in a million I could ever get you to trust me again, to even consider giving it another chance . . ."

She looked away, unable to meet his intense gaze. "I'm sorry, Bobby. It's too late."

He drew his hands away. "I figured." He stared into his cup of hot chocolate, still untouched. "Look. I know every couple who's ever broken up has said the same old thing: let's still be friends. But let's really try. I mean that, okay? You've been too important to me for too long for me to simply let you slip out of my life."

"All right."

"And if there's ever anything I can do . . . Well, you know the rest of the speech."

"I know it's more than a speech, Bobby. I know you mean it."

"I do, Miranda," he said, his voice hoarse. "I really do."

CHAPTER
6

Driving up along the Oregon coast to Portland early Saturday morning offered Miranda a welcome change. As she careened past the dramatic scenery, taking note of the powerful Cascade mountains on her right and the steep cliffs dropping into the Pacific Ocean on her left, she could feel the tension in her muscles slipping away. It was the perfect day for a long drive, the sun brilliant, the sky a pale, wintry shade of blue, and the clear air refreshingly cool. Her thoughts became clearer as she focused on the first rehearsal of *La Rose*.

It was only now when she was driving away from Overlook that she realized how overwhelmed she'd been by the events of the week—of the past few weeks, in fact. What a relief it was to leave all the complications of her day-to-day life behind, instead pouring her efforts into her great love: the theater. She grew more and more excited with each passing mile, grateful to have something else to concentrate on, something that was so important to her.

Standing in front of the Limelight Theater at five minutes before ten, Miranda felt a surge of excitement rising up inside her so strong that even her nervousness paled beside it. The only other time she'd been to this theater, after driving up with Elinor a few weeks earlier, she'd scarcely been able to believe she'd actually been invited to audition for Portland's finest acting troupe. This time, she was actually a part of it.

The theater was housed in a narrow building three stories high, made of red bricks. It was elegant, with its simple, clean lines. Colorful banners flying overhead announced the name of the theater company. Large posters advertising the season's productions framed the front entrance.

Striding into the theater, Miranda felt exhilarated. *This is the moment I've been waiting for*, she thought. *This feeling—the one that comes from doing something that really matters to me—is what I've craved.*

All her senses were heightened as she passed through the lobby and stepped into the theater. What a difference, compared to the first time she'd been inside! That time, only a few houselights had been on, bringing only dim illumination to the space with its walls and ceilings painted black. And there had been only one person there, Jeff Jordan.

This morning, the stage was alive with activity. The lights were bright, making the stage almost as bright as the sunlit day blazing outside. At least a dozen people chattered in groups, scanned scripts, stood drinking take-out coffee from paper cups. She recognized Camille and Ted and Evan, actors she'd met while having lunch at a Mexican restaurant with Jeff Jordan right after her audition. A team of lighting people were fussing with thick cables. Set up in the center of the stage was a long table, with folding metal chairs all around.

Even David Singer had already arrived. The director had an aura of theatricality about him. Dressed entirely in faded denim, the plump yet dignified man was surrounded by a trio of actors, gazing at him adoringly and hanging on to every word he spoke.

"Kind of like a scene from a play, isn't it?"

Miranda turned, surprised. "Jeff!" she exclaimed. "I was just wondering where you were."

"It looks as if this time, when David said ten sharp, he really meant it."

"I'm glad I made it on time. It's a long drive."

"Ah, yes. Up from the boondocks. What's the name of your quaint little hometown again? Overcast? Overdrive? Overextended?"

Miranda laughed. Her original observation about Jeff Jordan still held true: he *was* a puzzling young man, with a sense of humor she wasn't always certain she understood and an unnerving way of looking at her, as if he knew more about her than she wanted him to know. But she had to admit that she did enjoy his company. Something about him sparkled, as if he were just a little bit more alive than most other people.

"My 'quaint little hometown' is called Overlook," she told him, still laughing.

"That's right. Overlook. It sounds terribly colorful. High cliffs, tremendous mountains, lots of moss . . ." Suddenly he grew serious. "I'll have to drive down and check it out sometime."

Their conversation was cut short when David Singer clapped his hands for attention.

"All right, kiddies. It's show time. Let's get our little scripts and sit down in our little chairs and see if any of this makes sense."

Miranda watched as the rest of the actors headed toward the table, scripts in hand.

"Shall we?" said Jeff, lightly placing his hand on her waist.

The members of the troupe got right to work. Pushing coffee cups aside and tucking pocketbooks and other possessions out of the way, they began reading through the script. David Singer interrupted a few times, usually when someone missed a cue or failed to emphasize just the right word in the sentence.

Miranda was enthralled. Already the words

were jumping off the page, coming alive. While this was only the acting troupe's initial reading of the play, their finesse was already instilling the lines with meanings and nuances she hadn't picked up while reading it herself.

And then her heart began to pound. Her entrance was coming up, on the following page. Her part in the futuristic play, set in a cold and impersonal society, opened with a short monologue. In it, the character she played, Michelle, begged the leader, played by Jeff, for assistance in saving her father's land.

The moment finally came. Her cue came from a dark-haired woman in her twenties named Janine Mason, reading the part of his assistant.

"What is it you want of our leader?" Janine asked, her tone lofty.

"I am grateful for this chance to speak," Miranda began.

She could feel her stomach knot. Her voice sounded uncertain. Soft. Not at all convincing in the way a character as strong as the play's lead should have sounded. Yet she went on, trying to speak with more conviction. "I have come to ask for your help."

She stopped, nervously clearing her throat. "Uh, could I please start again?"

"Certainly." David Singer cast a perfunctory nod in her direction.

"I am grateful for this chance to speak. I have

come to ask for your help. My father is ill, and he cannot—"

"Miranda." The director spoke in such a low voice it was difficult for her to hear him over her pounding heart. "May I ask you a personal question?"

She swallowed hard. She could feel the eyes of the others burning into her. Ted, Camille, and of course Jeff. Miranda kept her own eyes fixed on the edge of the table.

"Yes," she said meekly.

"Have you ever wanted so desperately to help someone that you reached deep inside yourself and came up with a strength, a sense of yourself and your own power, that you never in your wildest dreams could even imagine existed?"

She thought for only a few seconds before responding. "Yes."

"All right, then. Listen to me, Miranda. I want you to recapture that feeling. Take a moment to think about it. Remember: you're acting not on your own behalf, not for yourself, but for someone else. Someone about whom you care very much. Perhaps even someone you love. Are you with me?"

She nodded.

"Good." David Singer was growing more and more enthusiastic. "Go with that feeling, Miranda. Bring it out. Feel it all over again. The pain. The desperation. And above all, the hope—the hope that you can help. That you can make a difference. That somehow, simply because you want it so badly, you can save this person, do for him what he can't do for himself.

"Feel *that*, Miranda, and project it. Make it come alive for the audience. Make it *real*."

Miranda closed her eyes. She was concentrating so hard that for the moment she forgot all about David Singer. And Jeff. And Ted and Camille and the other actors sitting around the table. She even forgot where she was.

For those few moments, all she knew was Garth. Garth, and her desperate longing, her yearning, to help him.

"I'm ready." She heard herself saying the words even before she knew she was about to speak. Opening her eyes, she saw that David Singer was staring at her intently.

"Go on," he said.

Miranda took a deep breath. She felt different, she realized. All her nervousness was gone. Her self-consciousness had also vanished.

In their place was strength, the kind of strength about which she now understood David Singer had spoken.

"I am grateful for this chance to speak." The voice she heard was clear and resonant. Confident. Determined. A voice she barely recognized as her own.

"I have come to ask for your help. My father

is ill, and he cannot hold on to his land unless he receives special dispensation. And so I beg of you, kind leader . . ."

She continued, speaking in the same unhalting manner. When she finally came to the end of the monologue, her posture was erect, her mannerisms those of a proud young woman intent on saving her father's land. Of doing for him what she knew he could not do for himself, not without her help. She experienced a sense of satisfaction unlike anything she had ever known.

And then, sitting back in her seat, she let her eyes travel down the page of the script she clutched in both hands. It was Jeff's turn to speak, Jeff in the role of the leader of the futuristic society. Yet there was only silence.

Confused, she glanced at him across the table. He was staring at her, as if transfixed. She looked at the others. As she went around the table, looking from one to the next, she saw the same look in everyone's eyes. It was a kind of awe. Admiration for what she had accomplished.

She realized then that she had won the respect of the members of a professional acting company.

Miranda could feel her cheeks reddening. Anxious to break the silence hovering over the room, she sputtered, "Uh, isn't it your turn, Commander Jeff?"

The whole cast burst out laughing.

"Let's all take a cue from Miranda, shall we?" said David Singer. "Make this play come alive. Pour yourselves into the souls of the characters you're playing. Allow the words to sing!"

Turning to Miranda, he said in a gentle voice, "Good work, Miranda."

It was after five by the time David Singer finally announced the rehearsal was over. Miranda was exhausted. The day had been exciting, but long. Except for a half-hour lunch break, during which a local delicatessen had delivered sandwiches and more of the coffee that was apparently an integral part of the rehearsal experience, the director and the actors had worked nonstop. The exhilaration she'd felt at the beginning gave way to the recognition that putting a play together was hard work.

Still, she could see that working with professionals made all the difference in the world. Once the rehearsals got going full-force, it would take no time at all to get the play into shape. Already she was dreaming about opening night.

Miranda was gathering up her things, preparing to leave the Limelight Theater and begin the long drive home, when she felt someone brush lightly against her arm.

"Well, well, well, Miranda. You certainly took the theatrical world by storm today." Jeff was at her side, standing close to her. His green eyes were fixed on her intently.

"Thank you," she replied. "Although the person who really deserves the praise is Mr. Singer. He's a good director, isn't he?"

"David's the best. But don't underestimate the importance of the raw material he's got to work with."

The smile Miranda cast him was sincere. "Thanks, Jeff. I have to admit, this turned out to be harder than I expected. Walking into an established professional theater company, the only outsider and the only amateur—"

"I'll do anything I can to make things easier for you. In fact, the offer I made on the phone still stands—"

"Jeff, *there* you are." Camille Bartlett came sashaying over to them, waving her arms in a histrionic motion. Miranda had gotten to know her a bit over lunch last month. She was an animated woman in her late forties or early fifties who was almost as dramatic offstage as she was onstage. "And here *you* are, Miranda. The two of you must join us for a celebratory dinner. We're all going over to Chatfield's. Say yes, now. I simply won't take no for an answer."

"Celebration?" Miranda blinked in confusion. "What are we celebrating?"

"Why, getting through the first grueling day of rehearsal, of course!"

Miranda had to admit, now that she was beginning to feel like one of the members of the troupe, she was reluctant for the day to end. Still, she'd assumed when she got home, even though she'd no doubt be tired from the long drive, she would go directly to Cedar Crest to tell Garth about the rehearsal. He'd been almost as excited as she was, making her promise she'd tell him all about it the first chance she got.

"You can't say no, Miranda," Jeff insisted.

"Well, I—"

"It's part of the initiation. Something all new members have to do." He winked at Camille.

"In that case—"

"Then it's settled." Playfully he put his arm around her shoulder. "I personally guarantee that you'll have a good time."

It's not as if Jeff and I are actually on a date, Miranda thought a few minutes later as she sat next to him at a small table in Chatfield's. It was a cozy coffeehouse with a fire in its stone fireplace, tattered books along the shelves that lined one entire wall, and posters from Broadway shows hanging on the others. Six other members of *La Rose*'s cast were also there, crowded around a corner table meant for four.

"The chocolate soufflé here is the best," Camille assured her, already checking the dessert menu. "You *do* like chocolate soufflé, don't you?"

"I've never had it," Miranda admitted, a bit sheepishly.

She glanced over at Jeff, expecting him to tease her. Instead, he gave her a warm smile. "Go ahead and order it. I promise you'll thank me. Of course, once you've tried it, your old-fashioned chocolate brownie will never be the same. "Besides," he added with a wink, "if you don't like it, I'll be more than happy to take it off your hands."

Miranda laughed. She was having fun. And, she was shocked to realize, that was due mostly to being with Jeff. The more time she spent with him, the more comfortable she felt around him. His sense of humor was actually growing on her. In fact, not only was she getting used to it, she was also beginning to enjoy it.

She couldn't help noticing the contrast between the way it felt being with Jeff . . . and with Garth. Her interactions with the young actor were so lighthearted, so easy, so free of conflict. Miranda couldn't remember the last time she'd laughed so hard or been so relaxed.

A wave of guilt washed over her. She shouldn't be thinking such thoughts. She felt as if she were betraying Garth. Garth was the boy she loved, the boy she was committed to. Her feelings for him went deep, far beyond what she'd ever felt for anyone. How could she even compare her passion for him with a casual flirtation with a boy like Jeff Jordan? She made a point of talking to all the members of the acting troupe, wanting to make sure Jeff didn't get the wrong idea.

It was close to nine o'clock when Miranda glanced at her watch. "Oh!" she cried. "I had no idea it was getting so late. I'm going to have to say good night."

"So soon?" Jeff looked genuinely disappointed.

"I still have a long drive back home," she reminded him. "The town of 'Overcast' is a long way off, remember?"

"You're welcome to stay at my place," Camille offered. "My couch is very comfortable, or so I've been told. It's certainly better than driving in the dark when you're overtired."

"Thank you, but I really should get going. Maybe some other time."

"I'll walk you out," Jeff offered, leaping out of his seat and helping her with her coat.

Outside, the night was cold, the sky a dark blanket covered with stars. Silence cloaked the streets as the two of them walked toward her car, Jeff close at her side. She was so aware of him. . . .

All of a sudden he reached over and took her hand.

"Miranda, I—"

"Jeff, I think there's something I need to tell you." She slipped her hand out of his. "Maybe I should have mentioned this sooner, but I wasn't sure. . . . There's somebody I'm seeing, down in

Overlook. Someone I care about very much. And, well, while I'm flattered by your interest in me, I just want you to know—"

"So I've got some competition, huh?" In the light from a nearby streetlamp, Miranda could see that Jeff was grinning. "Okay. Thanks for the tip. But there's something I need to tell *you*. I'm not the type of guy who gives up very easily. When I see something I want, I go after it. That's how I got so involved in acting."

He was standing very close to her, his green eyes glinting in the bright light. The dramatic shadows cast across his face made his features look even more handsome than usual. "And it's only fair to tell you that, when it comes to you, Miranda Campbell, I don't plan to give up without a fight."

CHAPTER
7

Miranda expected that after the demanding day of rehearsing in Portland and the long drive home at night, she'd be tired Sunday morning. Instead, she woke up early, buoyant over her success. She was energized even further by the bright sunlight streaming into her bedroom through the window, promising a magnificent day.

Garth, she thought. *I want to spend today with Garth.*

Suddenly anxiety gripped her. *I was supposed to see him last night,* she realized. Yet by the time she'd gotten back to Overlook, it was too late to go to Cedar Crest. . . .

As she pulled on jeans and a heavy fisherman's sweater, she tried to push her guilt aside. Instead, Miranda ruminated about how lately she and Garth had been spending too much of their precious time together dealing with adversity.

Where was the romance? she wondered. What had happened to those sweet moments that she still clung to so fondly, like dried flowers pressed in a book so they could be preserved forever? Suddenly Miranda longed to recapture that intoxicating feeling of being cloaked by their love, as if they were the only two people in the world.

Less than an hour later, she was standing at the front door of Cedar Crest, wearing a mysterious smile.

"Where are we going?" Garth asked.

"You'll see," Miranda replied. "Just make sure you wear comfortable clothes. Knee pads wouldn't hurt, either!"

She'd come up with the idea of going ice skating with Garth as she'd hurried up Winding Way. Her memories of her day at the rink with Bobby had been revitalized when she'd talked with him at the diner a few days earlier. She was anxious to have that same kind of fun all over again—this time with Garth.

Perhaps there was something else motivating her, she realized. She had to admit that seeing Bobby again, hearing him confess that he felt he'd made a mistake in breaking up with her— that he wished they could get back together again—had stirred up feelings she'd been trying to convince herself she no longer had. But she was saddened by having to say good-bye to a chapter of her life that had been so tender and innocent. And the best way she knew of to banish that sadness was to relive one of the scenes that had once brought her such joy.

The ice-skating rink in Carlton, a few miles south of Norton, was crowded on this brisk Sunday afternoon. Music with a clear, steady beat was blaring over the loudspeaker as Miranda plopped down on a bench, her rented skates in hand.

"I've never seen you on the ice," she remarked to Garth as she laced up her skate. "Are you good?"

"Well, I haven't done much ice skating," he said thoughtfully. "But I'm pretty strong, and I'm well-coordinated, and I've got a good sense of balance. . . . I suppose you could say I move with the grace of an animal."

Miranda laughed. How good it felt, joking together! Just for today, she wanted to forget all about the complications in their lives. To relax, for a change, to take time to step back and simply have fun. They needed this. To get away from the struggle that had occupied so much energy, so much emotion, from the very start. To *enjoy* each other's company, taking pleasure in simply being together.

"Come on. I'll race you around the rink!" Miranda called. Already she was stepping onto the ice, taking a few seconds to get her bearings and then skimming across the smooth surface with ease.

Within seconds she felt Garth's strong arm around her waist. "Thought you were dealing with a greenhorn, hmmm?" he said teasingly, his mouth next to her ear, his breath causing a chill to run down her spine. The way he'd come upon her so unexpectedly made her flesh tingle. "As the old saying goes, 'You ain't seen nothing yet.'"

She reached out to take his arm, but before she could, he took off on his own, racing around the rink with such speed and grace that many of the other skaters turned around to watch him. He hadn't been exaggerating when he'd so offhandedly referred to his strength and coordination and sense of balance. He was an excellent skater. Miranda watched him, spellbound, as he conquered the ice.

Finally he caught up with her, once again encircling her waist with his powerful arm.

"Not bad, huh?" he said lightly.

"You were wonderful!" she breathed.

Garth shrugged. "It's fun to show off every once in a while. But I'd much rather skate with you."

For the next hour, Miranda and Garth skated together, the strength and grace of one complementing that of the other. Moving together, responding to the pulsing rhythm of the music in the same way, was instinctive. They skated in time to the music, trying different steps and combinations, laughing so hard that they collapsed against each other when they couldn't

quite manage to pull it off. Miranda couldn't remember the last time she'd had so much fun.

"We make a good team," Garth commented
when the two of them finally perfected a particularly difficult move they'd been working on, a
combination she'd picked up watching professional ice skaters on television.

"I think so," she returned. Glancing up at
him, she saw that his blue eyes were burning
into hers with even more intensity than usual.
She realized then that he hadn't only been talking about ice skating.

"I need a break," she finally announced. All
of a sudden she was weary, her muscles rebelling
against the arduous demands that had been
made upon them.

She led him over to a bench near the concession stand.

"You sit here, m'lady, and rest your delicate
frame," said Garth. "How does hot chocolate
sound?"

Miranda smiled. "It sounds perfect."

He reappeared a few minutes later, bearing
two paper cups of hot chocolate topped with
whipped cream.

"Careful. It's hot," he said, sitting down beside her.

Miranda rested her cup on the bench beside
her, then leaned her head against his shoulder.
"This is so wonderful," she said with a sigh. "I'm

glad we came here today. We needed to get away, to be together like this, just the two of us—"

"Hey, there's that guy!" a high-pitched voice suddenly squealed.

Surprised, Miranda looked up. Three small children, no more than seven or eight years old, were standing in front of her and Garth. The one in the middle was pointing.

"Yeah, he's the one," the little girl next to him agreed.

Miranda smiled. She assumed they were complimenting Garth on his superb performance on the ice. She was about to speak when the third child, the smallest, piped up.

"*He's* the *werewolf*!"

Panic rose inside Miranda. All of a sudden the rink began to spin, the colors of the skaters' clothes whirling before her eyes in a confusing, constantly changing pattern. The music was deafeningly loud, so loud she could barely hear herself think.

"Miranda?" she heard Garth say calmly. "What are these kids talking about?"

"I'll tell you what we're talking about." Boldly the boy in the center stepped forward. "We know all about what happened. Some crazy guy who thinks he's a werewolf has been running around the woods, attacking people!"

"And you're him!" the smallest child cried.

"Garth, let's get out of here." Miranda was already on her feet, pulling him by the hand. "I'll explain later. Please, let's just leave!"

She headed toward the door, the hot chocolate forgotten.

"Amy Patterson is the one behind this," Miranda explained as she drove away from the ice-skating rink, so upset she was veering around corners much too quickly. "She's come up with this crazy new theory. I've known all along she could be trouble. I just had no idea how *much*."

Even clutching the steering wheel so tightly that her knuckles were white didn't stop her from trembling. She was still shaken by the children's unexpected verbal attack. Now she wished she'd taken a stronger stand instead of simply fleeing.

She knew she and Garth wouldn't be able to keep running away forever.

"How did she figure it out?" Garth asked, his voice quiet. He was sitting beside her in the front seat, staring out the window. His shoulders were slumped, his entire posture one of defeat.

"She didn't. Amy heard about some psychiatric disorder called lycanthropy. It's a syndrome where the patient thinks he—"

"You don't have to explain," Garth said in the same monotone. "I already know all about it."

Miranda cast him a sidelong glance. "At least she doesn't know the real truth," she said, trying her best to sound optimistic.

"No, she doesn't," he replied, his gaze still fixed on the passing scenery. "At least, not yet."

After Miranda had left him at Cedar Crest, Garth stood in the garden for a long time. The scene at the ice-skating rink continued to haunt him. Just when he had let his guard down—letting himself enjoy being with Miranda, doing the kinds of things he had always longed to do but hadn't dared—he had been reminded that, for him, such freedom didn't exist.

All his life he had known what it meant to be alone. Even as a child, Garth had held back, sensing he was different . . . and wanting to keep the others from finding out.

Miranda's mention of the word "lycanthropy" had brought it all back. Of course he knew about the syndrome. After the first time he had shapeshifted, he had gone to Portland's main library, determined to find some explanation for what had happened to him.

Even more important, he was certain he could find a way to keep it from ever happening to him again.

There, in the dusty stacks of the basement, poring over the thick tomes in the psychiatry section, he had first come across the word. It came from the Greek language, he'd discovered, *lykos* meaning wolf and *anthropos* meaning man.

Wolf-Man. Just seeing the word had caused Garth's heart to pound.

Eagerly he'd read, sitting on the basement floor of the library for hours, dragging book after book off the shelf and reading every word he could find, struggling to understand the complicated medical terms.

The one word that stood out on the page most was *insanity.*

Am I insane? he had wondered. Have I lost my mind, believing that I have the ability to change into a wolf?

Yet even in that thought he had found comfort. An explanation—*any* explanation—was better than being shrouded in confusion.

The very next time the moon was full, exactly twenty-nine days later, he had clung to the possibility that what he thought was happening to him was in actuality only in his mind. That evening, he had hidden in the basement of his home. Before going downstairs, he brought a big mirror into the cellar, leaning it against the wall so he could clearly see his own image reflected. He also brought a Polaroid camera, keeping it next to him.

It's all in your mind, he told himself, growing more agitated as he waited. *You're simply imagining the whole thing. It said so in the medical textbooks . . . and tonight you'll be able to prove it to yourself.*

When he'd felt the change begin, both dread

and excitement washed over him. It *was* happening again. The moon was full, and the transformation was coming upon him for the second time.

Things were proceeding precisely the way he'd expected, in the same manner in which they'd occurred before. His skin prickled, his nerves grew more sensitive than usual. His senses became substantially more acute, as well. Suddenly he could hear things he'd never heard from the basement before. His mother, moving about on the second floor, the water moving through the pipes, even sounds from outdoors. And his sense of smell was so strong he could hardly bear it. The odor of mildew in the basement, the scent of a mouse crouching behind the wall . . . he picked up the most subtle smells imaginable. He could feel the room around him fading, as if he were no longer a part of the world in the way he had been before.

He could also feel his body changing. His fingernails quickly grew into sharp claws right before his eyes. And golden fur covered his entire body.

It's not real! This is not really happening. . . .

Garth turned then, confronting the mirror head-on. And his heart constricted. The changes he was experiencing were reflected in the glass. The alteration of his body and his head, the appearance of the fur—as thick as that of a real wolf—it was all right there in front of him.

"No!" he cried out loud. Already his voice had grown deep, the single word that shattered the silence of the room sounding more like an animal's howl than the cry of a boy.

Quickly he snatched up the camera. Still standing in front of the mirror, he snapped a picture of what was reflected there. The few seconds it took for the photograph to develop seemed an eternity. As he waited, he continued to stare at the mirror, watching the changes overtake him.

And then the picture took form. Garth grabbed it, staring at it in the basement's pale light.

In the photograph, below the bright patch made by the camera's flash, was the figure of a young man.

At least the being in the picture was partly a young man. Even more so the creature captured on film looked like a wolf.

He understood then that he hadn't imagined it. The change was real. Shapeshifting was not something that went on only in his head . . . it truly happened.

Once again, Garth let out a cry. This time, there was no mistaking the sound that escaped his throat. It was a howl . . . the mournful howl of the werewolf.

And then his awareness faded. The boy was no more; the mind inside the beast's body was that of an animal. The photograph fell to the floor, and the massive wolf padded toward an open window, stealing out into the night.

That scene had occurred three years earlier. Yet as he thought about it, replaying it in his mind, Garth experienced the same feelings he had felt that night. Fear, that he was out of control, his actions governed by someone—or something—outside of himself. Self-loathing, that he was powerless to keep himself from becoming what he so detested.

Most of all, on that night as well as today, Garth experienced utter hopelessness.

The next morning at school, Miranda, too, was still troubled by the scene at the ice-skating rink. All she'd wanted was a chance to get away, to be with Garth without any interference from the rest of the world.

Even that was becoming impossible.

She wanted to be alone. And so Miranda made a point of avoiding the people she knew, coming into the school building at the last possible moment and keeping her eyes down. Still, she knew she couldn't hide all day.

That truth became more evident than ever when she walked into her first-period English class. Dave Falco was sitting on her desk.

"Hello, Dave," she said in a soft, controlled voice.

"Good morning, Miranda." His singsong tone was teasing, but the look in his dark eyes was hard. "I've been waiting for you."

"So I see." She pulled out her chair and sat down. "I hope you don't intend to sit there the whole period. It's going to be a little difficult seeing what Mr. Wexler writes on the blackboard."

"Oh, I'm not staying. I just wanted to pass on a little piece of news. You might say it's a new development." He stared at her for a long time before adding, "I have a feeling you and your boyfriend will really enjoy this."

"I can hardly wait."

Dave stuck his chin up in the air. "It's about Mark. You remember Mark, don't you?"

Miranda glanced up, surprised. "Of course I do. I heard he was due to be released from the hospital any day now."

"Yeah, that's what the doctors thought. That is, until the infection set in."

"Infection?"

"You heard me. Those second-degree burns of his aren't their main concern anymore—now that he's got a staph infection."

"I—I'm sorry to hear that." The regret reflected in her voice was sincere.

"Yeah, you should be."

"How much longer is he going to have to stay in the hospital?"

"You still don't get it, do you?" Dave hissed, his eyes burning into hers. "Mark could *die*."

* * *

Miranda was in a daze for the rest of the morning. She was contemplating going home, admitting that she was no longer capable of handling all the adversity that was being thrown her way. But Elinor was going to be reading a scene from *A Doll's House* in theater class, and she wanted to be on hand to lend moral support.

Sitting in the school auditorium, she was barely able to concentrate on Elinor's recitation of the play's main character, Nora's, most famous scenes. All she could think about as she stared at the stage from one of the back rows was how she was caught in a spiral, one that kept dragging her further and further down.

Where will all this end? she thought, on the verge of tears. *How can we ever triumph over this terrible misfortune? I can't escape it. It's everywhere I go. Everyone is turning against us. . . .*

She sat up a little straighter, trying her hardest to concentrate on the scene being performed onstage.

"How was I?" At the end of the period, as Miranda hurried out of the auditorium, Elinor was suddenly at her side. Her hazel eyes were sparkling.

"You were terrific." A stab of guilt shot through Miranda. She'd barely heard a word of Elinor's reading. She'd been too lost in thought . . . too absorbed in her own problems.

Elinor sighed. "Did you *really* think I did a good job?"

"You're a wonderful actress, Elinor." This time, at least, Miranda's words were truthful.

"Miranda," Elinor said seriously, once they were out in the corridor, "are you all right?"

"Of course." Miranda replied a little too quickly. "Why wouldn't I be all right?"

"I don't know. You just seem kind of . . . distant."

"I guess I've just got a lot on my mind these days. The rehearsals up in Portland, the party this Friday night . . ." She cast Elinor an apologetic look. "I'm sorry if I seem far away. I don't mean to be."

"I know." Elinor hesitated, as if there were more she wanted to say. But then she smiled. "I can hardly wait until your party. It's going to be just the thing to put everybody in a festive mood. Not everybody is, you know."

"What do you mean?"

"You haven't heard? There's talk around town about canceling Overlook's holiday celebrations. The winter carnival, the Christmas caroling—"

"That's terrible! Why on earth would anyone want to cancel all that?"

"Because of the attacks," Elinor explained. "Some people are saying it would be disrespectful to go all out this year with Andy and Corinne's attacker still on the loose."

"I feel as bad as anybody about what's been going on," Miranda said, "but I can't see how celebrating the holidays would be disrespectful toward the Davises and the Swensens."

"Unfortunately, Mrs. Swensen doesn't agree with you. She's one of the ringleaders of this 'movement.' There's going to be a meeting next week so people can air their views on whether or not to call a moratorium on all the holiday festivities until this is settled once and for all. Maybe you should go."

"I might do that."

"In the meantime, I want to go on record as saying that I, for one, can't wait to get totally swept up in the Christmas spirit! I already got a good start on my shopping last month, when I went up to Portland with you for your audition. But I haven't started wrapping the presents I bought yet. I'm thinking of your party as the official beginning of the Christmas season."

"I hope my little get-together lives up to your expectations!"

"Oh, I'm sure it will. And if you need any help, I happen to be an expert at stringing popcorn and unraveling strings of Christmas-tree lights and—"

Elinor stopped mid-sentence. "Hi, Corinne," she said, looked over Miranda's shoulder and smiling warmly.

Miranda turned around and saw Corinne coming toward them. She was looking better and better each day, she noted. The color was slowly coming back into her face and some of her usual animation was returning.

"Hello, Elinor. Hi, Miranda."

"What are you up to?" Miranda asked congenially.

Corinne grimaced. "Hiding from Amy Patterson, mostly."

"Why? What's she up to now?"

"Oh, she's been badgering me with this ridiculous new 'theory' of hers."

"Oh, really?" Miranda swallowed hard, remembering what Selina had told her. "I think I've heard about this."

"She keeps insisting my attacker was a psychopath, someone stricken with this mental illness she says is called lye . . . lycan . . ."

"Lycanthropy?" Miranda offered.

"Yes, that's it." Corinne sighed. "Apparently she's been reading a book about it. And she won't let up—at least, not with me. It sounds as if she's determined to get me to forget the idea that the attacker was an animal. I can't for the life of me figure out why."

"She'll get bored with it eventually," Elinor said soothingly. "Amy strikes me as the type who never sticks with anything for very long."

"I hope you're right. If I hear one more thing about werewolves and full moons and the hour of the wolf—"

"The hour of the wolf?" Miranda asked guardedly. "What's that?"

"Oh, just another part of Amy's weird little campaign. She told me that's how people used to refer to four o'clock in the morning."

"What does it mean?" asked Elinor.

Corinne shrugged. "Beats me. I just wish she'd go find somebody else to pick on."

"Well, at least she won't be at Miranda's party Friday night," Elinor said. "Since she and Bobby are no longer an item, I assume she's off the guest list, right?"

"Unless she decides to crash," Corinne joked.

"I hope not!" Miranda exclaimed. "I'm hoping for a nice, calm evening, one with as little unplanned excitement as possible!"

The night before the party, Miranda scribbled away in her diary for close to an hour. It was late and she was tired, yet the words kept flowing. She had started out writing about her growing anticipation about Friday night's get-together. It was going to be fun, hosting a holiday party. The decorations were in place, the menu was planned, the dress she wanted to wear was hanging in the closet, fresh from the dry cleaners.

But as she filled page after page in her journal, she also expressed her apprehensions. Some of them were rooted in her nervousness. Whether or not people would feel at ease, whether there would be enough food . . . whether her guests would have fun.

But there were also more substantial fears haunting her. First and foremost was Garth. He had spent little time with her friends from school. The party Bobby had thrown back in November had ended disastrously. That night Amy and Selina had pounced, going out of their way to comment on how "mysterious" he was—and how much of a coincidence it was that the attacks on two Overlook students had occurred right after his arrival in town.

She hoped this time would be different. She desperately wanted Garth to feel comfortable with her friends . . . and for them, in turn, to accept him.

Then there was Bobby. When she'd originally invited him, she'd expected him to come with Amy. Now he'd be coming alone. She was nervous about whether or not he and Garth would get along. She didn't expect there to be any hard feelings, at least not on the surface, but she couldn't help worrying.

As she wrote, however, lying on her stomach with her head bent over her diary, all her fears came pouring out onto the pages of the book. Her concerns over Garth—not only his well-being, but his safety, as well. Her worries about the changes she was going through herself, now that she'd truly fallen in love for the first time, now that she'd experienced shapeshifting herself . . . now that she'd come to understand the odds she was up against.

And, as had been the case more and more lately, the disturbing question of whether or not the love she and Garth shared would in the end be strong enough to withstand the trials she knew still lay ahead of them.

Finally she put down her pen, exhausted. She meant to rest for only a moment, to close her eyes. . . .

And then she was running through the forest, wild and free. She experienced the same exhilaration she had felt while shapeshifting. But this time she was herself, a young woman running through the woods, wearing only the flowing white nightgown she had donned before going to bed.

Even though her feet were bare, she felt no pain as she sprinted over jagged rocks and branches covered with sharp twigs. The leafless trees told her it was winter, yet the air was not cold.

Even more remarkable was how powerful she was. She crossed the forest floor in great strides, each step advancing her another five or six feet. And she was traveling quickly, at such a great speed that she could feel the wind whistling past her.

As she ran, she gradually became aware that she was clutching something tightly in her hand. Surprised, she glanced down.

It was the knife.

She stopped. Glancing around, she saw she

was at the edge of the cliff—the cliff that hung over the treacherous stretch of beach called Devil's End. The wind was blowing furiously, rising off the violent waters of the Pacific Ocean. She could hear the waves crashing far below, battling with the sharp boulders that lay in wait.

She knew instinctively what she had to do. Raising the knife high into the air, with all her might she struck downward, stabbing at the air. Once, twice, three times . . .

And then she was lying awake in her bed, the light still on, her diary and her pen beside her. Her heart was pounding and she was breathing heavily. Her right hand was clenched into a tight fist, her fingers clasped together so tightly her nails cut into her flesh. She was making a stabbing motion.

She stopped, relaxing her fingers. It took her a few seconds to understand that she had drifted off to sleep. Checking the clock, she saw it was four o'clock in the morning.

The hour of the wolf.

She was shaking, she realized, as if in response to an icy gust of wind. Yet the windows in her room were closed and the blankets were pulled up all around her.

It hadn't been real, she told herself. It was only a nightmare, a terrible nightmare.

Or was it?

CHAPTER
8

"How do I look?"

Miranda pirouetted for her mother, who was standing in the doorway of her bedroom. After spending the afternoon preparing for the party—baking, decorating, fussing with a hundred little details—she'd taken more than an hour to dress. She'd luxuriated in a warm bubble bath, taken great care with her makeup, agonized over her hair. Tonight was a special night, and she wanted everything to be just so.

"You look lovely," Mrs. Campbell told her, smiling.

"This was such a great idea, Mom." Miranda wrapped her arms around her mother and gave her a big hug. "It was really fun, planning this party with you."

"It was fun for me, too, honey. It's been a long time since you and I have worked on something like this together. And I just know this is going to be a special night for you."

After she'd left, Miranda stood in front of the mirror hanging above her dresser, wanting to check her appearance one more time before going downstairs to wait for her guests to arrive. She reached down and smoothed her dress, a rich shade of royal-blue velvet. The neckline was low, gently scooped so that it showed off the creamy skin of her throat and her shoulders. The skirt gently skimmed her slender hips.

Her hair was pulled back on the sides and fastened in back with a silver hair ornament. The shiny metal complemented the Native American jewelry she was wearing, the three pieces she'd gotten at a local craft fair years earlier. She loved the earrings and the bracelet, inscribed in black with an intriguing geometric pattern.

But it was the necklace that was her favorite. As she fastened it around her neck, she admired the tiny animals, hand-carved from different colored stones, that dangled from the delicate silver chain.

Putting it on, fingering the head of the wolf carved from the unusual black stone swirled with murky green, she found her thoughts drifting. She was picturing the forest, dark and shadowy, imagining how it would feel to be there, sniffing the cold winter air, picking up the scent of an animal far in the distance, running stealthily over rocks and bogs. . . .

Tonight she didn't want to think about any of that. Still looking at her reflection, she shook her head hard, trying to banish all thoughts except those of gleeful anticipation. In a few minutes, she reminded herself, her guests would begin arriving. This was a night to have fun. After brushing on a little more blush, Miranda went downstairs, determined to put herself in a party mood.

She glanced around the living room with a critical eye, wanting to make sure everything was just right. A fire roared in the fireplace, and the mantelpiece above it was looped with pine garlands. Red candles glowed from every corner. Stacked on the piano was a pile of presents, wrapped in shiny red and green paper. But the room's centerpiece was the Christmas tree, a tall Scotch pine, full and fragrant and perfectly shaped, covered with ornaments that had been in the family since Miranda was a child.

Mrs. Campbell came out of the kitchen, a tray of Christmas cookies in her hand. She placed it on the dining-room table with all the other refreshments, then came into the living room. Slinging her arm around Miranda's shoulders, she glanced around appraisingly.

"It looks nice, doesn't it?" Her eyes were glowing, reflecting the light from the candles.

Before Miranda had a chance to respond, the doorbell rang.

It was Selina, dressed in bright green tights

and a red tunic that gave her an elflike appearance. A row of colorful bangle bracelets ran up one arm. In her hand was a huge candy cane.

"Let the festivities begin!" she cried, prancing into the room. Abruptly she stopped. "Hey, this is supposed to be my grand entrance. Where is everybody?"

"You're the first to arrive," Miranda told her, laughing.

"Who's coming?" Selina asked. "You didn't invite Amy, did you?"

"No."

"Good. But Corinne's coming, right?"

"I hope so."

"And Garth?"

Miranda was silent for a moment. She was still worried about how he'd fit in.

Please, please, let things go smoothly tonight, she thought, her stomach tightening.

Forcing herself to smile brightly at Selina, she said, "Of course Garth is coming. He could hardly wait."

The doorbell rang again. It was Elinor, bearing a tray of gingerbread men. She was followed by a group of five of Miranda's friends who'd driven over together. From that point on, the guests continued to pour in. Selina took on the role of unofficial cohostess, Miranda was more than a little relieved to note, telling people where to put their coats and pointing them in the direction of the refreshments.

"Make sure you have a piece of that giant candy cane," Selina quipped. "It must serve forty!"

When Miranda answered the door and found Bobby standing on the threshold, she was suddenly tongue-tied.

"Hello, Bobby," she said. She hesitated, then leaned forward and kissed him lightly on the cheek. "I'm glad you could make it."

"Thanks. I am too." As he stepped inside, he reached into his pocket and pulled out a small box, wrapped in silver paper and tied with a red ribbon.

"For me?" Miranda's surprise was genuine.

"Merry Christmas, Miranda. I know it's early, but . . . Go ahead, open it."

Inside the box was a necklace made of dried marionberries strung together.

"It's nothing fancy, I know. But I figured it's the thought that counts." Shyly, Bobby added, "I made it myself."

"Oh, Bobby. It's wonderful." Miranda couldn't help being touched by the sentiments behind the simple gift. As children, Bobby and Miranda had spent many hours roaming the fields and the mountainsides surrounding Overlook, exploring and examining the marvels of nature . . . and gathering marionberries. "I'll treasure it always."

"Well," Bobby said, his voice suddenly hearty,

"guess I'll go on inside. Mind if I get myself something to drink?"

"Of course not. Help yourself." As he was walking into the dining room, she called after him, "Bobby?"

"Hmmm?" He glanced over his shoulder.

"Thank you."

He made a face. "For a bunch of berries strung together?"

"For remembering."

For a few minutes, Miranda chatted with Laura and Dawn, two of the people from her theater class who had come. They wanted to know about what it was like rehearsing at the Limelight.

When the doorbell rang one more time, she flung it open and found Garth standing on the front steps. He was wearing a broad smile and his blue eyes were shining. His arms were outstretched, palms upward.

"Look what I brought for you," he said in a soft voice, tilting his face upward. "Merry Christmas, my love."

It took Miranda a few seconds to understand what he meant. All around him, snow had just begun falling gently. Fat white flakes tumbled down from the sky, dusting the shoulders of his gray suede jacket, dotting his tousled blond hair.

Looking past him, she saw that a layer of white was beginning to blanket the grass. The most ordinary objects were suddenly transformed: bushes converted into gnomes, branches shimmering, rocks whose jagged edges were softened with cottony tufts. The world was silent and still, a magical place.

"Oh, Garth!" she cried. "The first snow of the season!"

"For you," he replied. "It's all for you."

He came inside, taking hold of her arm and silently leading her into the kitchen. Once they were alone, he folded his arms around her and drew her close.

"I love you, Miranda," he whispered in her ear. "I'm yours. And I want you to be mine."

"Yes," she replied, so out of breath it was difficult for her to speak. "Forever."

When he leaned over and kissed her, she felt a passion emanating from him that she had never before experienced. He held her so close she could feel his heartbeat.

Yet there was something else: an intensity that seemed rooted in desperation.

"Garth, are you all right?" she asked, pulling back.

"I love you so much, Miranda. I need you. Sometimes I'm overwhelmed by the way I feel about you. But lying underneath it is fear . . . fear that our love will dissolve."

He shook his head slowly. "Sometimes I think I'm being selfish in loving you so much. That I

should have followed my initial instincts and
stayed away.

"I'm cursed, Miranda. Look how it's affecting
you. Last Sunday, at the ice-skating rink . . .
Already people are turning against you—"

"Amy has been against me since the beginning," Miranda insisted. "As for everyone else, it
doesn't matter what they think about me . . . or
you. You and I together: that's all that matters."

"Ah, Miranda. I only wish I could be sure—"

"Ooops. Sorry." Selina had just poked her
head in the door.

"It's all right," Miranda assured her. "We
were just talking."

Selina only raised her eyebrows. "I just
wanted to tell you about the great idea I came
up with. It's the perfect way of getting a holiday
party off to a great start."

Miranda waved her hand in the air. "Be my
guest."

Leading Garth back into the living room, she
heard Selina saying, "Hey, everybody. How about
singing some Christmas carols?" Selina was already at the piano. "Does everybody know the
words to 'The First Noel?'"

Garth, still holding her hand tightly, glanced
over at Miranda. "Looks like the party's getting
underway. Shall we join in?"

Miranda perched on the arm of the couch,
with Garth sitting at her feet, cross-legged on

the floor. It wasn't long before she was wrapped up in singing all her favorite Christmas carols. Selina was an enthusiastic conductor, her colorful bangle bracelets clanging musically as she led the group. Miranda was so absorbed in the burgeoning holiday spirit that she forgot there was one guest missing.

It wasn't until the doorbell sounded, its shrill ring cutting through the group's enthusiastic rendition of "Deck the Halls," that she remembered.

"Corinne!" she cried, hopping off the arm of the couch. "I was hoping she'd make it tonight."

She threw her arms around Corinne as soon as she opened the door. "I'm so glad to see you," she said sincerely, giving her a tight squeeze.

"Sorry I'm late." Corinne stepped inside, unwrapping the wool muffler tucked around her throat. "It sounds like everybody's having fun."

"Selina got the ball rolling. You know what a ham she can be. Come on in."

Miranda led the way, with Corinne not far behind. Everyone had just finished singing "Deck the Halls," their rousing rendition charging the room with energy.

"Hey, everybody," said Miranda. "Look who's here."

The guests looked over expectantly, their faces lighting up. There was a chorus of hellos.

"Hi, Corinne!" cried Laura Ames. She waved from the corner of the room, where she was leaning on the piano. "Glad you could make it."

"That's a gorgeous sweater," Elinor added sincerely. She was in front of the fireplace, curled up on a small wooden bench. "Red's a really good color on you."

"Thanks." Corinne hesitated in the doorway of the living room, smiling shyly as she surveyed the faces.

And then her smile faded. Her gaze had settled on Garth, still sitting cross-legged on the floor in front of the couch. Instantly her eyes grew wide.

"No!" she shrieked, recoiling. "*No!*"

"Corinne!" Miranda cried. "What's happening? Talk to me!"

But she didn't seem to have heard. She backed away, still staring at Garth, her face stricken. And then, turning, she ran out of the house.

"I hope she's all right," Mrs. Campbell said, her forehead creased with worry. She was sitting opposite Miranda at the kitchen table early the next morning, an untouched cup of coffee sitting in front of her.

"I do too." Miranda sighed. "Her mother said she went straight to bed last night, after she got home. That was probably the best thing for her to do."

"I suppose it was simply too soon for her to be back in the swing of things. I imagine suffering a shock the way Corinne did must leave its mark for a very long time." Mrs. Campbell shook her head thoughtfully. "Well, perhaps a good night's sleep has helped her put things into perspective."

"I intend to find out," Miranda told her. "First thing after breakfast, I'm heading over to her house."

Mrs. Davis's lips were drawn into a straight line as she answered the door.

"I'm not sure she should be having visitors," Corinne's mother said. "But since you've gone to all the trouble of coming over—"

"I won't stay long," Miranda promised. "I just want to make sure she's all right."

She found Corinne in the same position she'd been in the last time she'd visited her at her house, a week and a half earlier, sitting on the edge of her bed. That other time, Miranda had been relieved to see a spark in her eyes, however slight. This time, she saw only signs of defeat.

"Corinne?" she called in a soft voice, stepping into her bedroom. The blinds had been opened slightly, letting in the smallest bit of light.

"I'm surprised you're still talking to me," Corinne returned.

"Of course I'm still talking to you! Why wouldn't I be?"

"You mean aside from the fact that I ruined your party?"

"You didn't ruin it. We were all upset by what happened, but everyone still stayed until after midnight."

"I know. I heard all about it from Selina. She called me this morning. So did half a dozen other kids."

"See that? Everyone was concerned."

"Who knows what they *really* think?" Corinne said morosely. "I wouldn't be surprised if they all think I'm crazy."

"Of course they don't think that. They just figured it was too soon for you to be—"

"Maybe they're right," Corinne went on, ignoring what she'd said. "Maybe I *am* crazy."

She looked at Miranda with a mournful expression. "I can't explain it. All I know is that as soon as I looked at Garth, something in me just snapped. I was overcome with this feeling of terror. It was like nothing I've ever felt before. Except once . . ."

Miranda swallowed. She was sure she knew what she was referring to. And she was just as certain she knew why.

Corinne had obviously linked Garth to her attack. That night, that terrible night, he had been in the form of a wolf. A werewolf. Nothing about him had looked the same, except the animal's thick golden fur, the same color as his hair, and the eyes.

Miranda was certain Corinne had not reacted so strongly to seeing Garth again for the first time since her attack because of any physical resemblance. It was something that went much deeper. Her response had come from her unconcious mind.

Even so, Miranda understood that the scene between Corinne and Garth, one that had been witnessed by so many people, could be harmful to him.

"Oh, Corinne, you've suffered such a terrible shock," Miranda said, sitting on the bed beside her and putting her arm around her shoulders. "You've got to give yourself time."

"Is that really all I need?" Corinne asked, her voice as meek as a little girl's.

After she left Corinne's house, Miranda headed for Cedar Crest. After the terrible scene the night before, Garth had been subdued for the rest of the evening.

On the surface, he'd done a good job of acting as if nothing were wrong, and she suspected that he'd managed to fool the other guests. But they didn't know him the way she did. She had seen the look in his eyes. The look of fear, like that of a hunted animal.

She'd longed to take him aside, to comfort him. Yet she knew only too well that the words that could truly take away his fears did not exist.

She was snapped back to the present as she caught her first glimpse of Cedar Crest. Miranda was startled by how sad the mansion looked. It was cast in shadows, the oblique light of morning dulling its colors and draping its odd angles in darkness. It was crumbling, she saw, its once-enlivened appearance giving way to decay. The shutters drooped, the gray facade was cracked. Weeds sprouted among the bricks lining the walkway.

Even the air surrounding the mansion was stale. The birds had again fallen silent. A feeling of lifelessness, of gloom, hung over the entire house.

I am responsible, she thought, a sense of doom coming over her. *Once my love for Garth revitalized this place. Now my dalliance with shapeshifting, my flirtation with evil, has brought sorrow and decay.*

For a moment Miranda was overwhelmed, torn by her love for Garth—the purest, most uplifting feeling she had ever had—and her yearning to cross over to the other side, a craving so base, so despicable, she could barely bring herself to admit to it.

Those two conflicting emotions were such utter contradictions, yet they were both so strong that she could ignore neither of them.

More than ever she longed to see Garth, wanting to forget that side of her she had already grown to despise.

"Garth?" she cried, standing outside.

There was no response, only the empty echo of her own voice. The front door did not open to bid her welcome.

She pulled it open herself, meeting with great resistance.

Was it possible she was no longer welcome here? she wondered.

Still she forged ahead, stepping into the foyer.

"Garth?" she called. "Garth, where are you?"

Once again, there was no sound except that of her own voice. It sounded hollow. Frightened. Above all, terribly alone.

Miranda knew, in a sudden flash of understanding, what living her life without Garth would be like. And the wrenching pain in her chest in the place where her heart used to be told her that the pain and the emptiness would make it barely worth enduring.

"*Garth!*"

This time, her cry was a mournful wail. It was a sound that rose up from her soul, a sound filled with desperation.

CHAPTER
9

"Going out tonight?" Miranda glanced up from book she was reading. She lay curled up on the living-room couch, a hand-crocheted afghan pulled up over her. Her mother had just come downstairs, dressed in one of her favorite outfits. There was an unmistakable glow on her cheeks.

Mrs. Campbell smiled. "Your father should be here to pick me up any minute. What about you? Are you going out? It *is* Saturday night."

"No. Actually, I'm looking forward to a quiet evening at home." She held up her book.

"Not a bad idea. It's such a nasty evening." Mrs. Campbell pulled back the curtain and peered outside. "It looks like there's a storm brewing. Why don't you light a fire in the fireplace?" She shivered, then let the curtain drop. "I almost envy you, staying in on an evening like this."

"You'll have fun," Miranda assured her.

"Where are you and Daddy going tonight?"

"Oh, just to a movie, over in Norton. Maybe we'll stop for a cup of coffee afterward."

"To give the two of you a chance to talk?" Miranda asked hopefully.

"Yes, as a matter of fact." Her mother came over and sat on the edge of the couch. She placed her hand on her daughter's. "It probably sounds funny to you, the way he and I are making time to get to know each other all over again."

Miranda's voice was soft as she said, "It doesn't sound funny at all."

After her mother had left, Miranda put down her book, unable to concentrate on the words on the page. She was still concerned about Garth. She knew him well enough to suspect he was avoiding her, that he was still so upset about what had happened at the party he couldn't face her. And while her first instinct had been to find him, she realized now that it was important that she respect his need to be alone.

But that didn't stop her from worrying about him. She felt for him in a way she had never before felt for another human being. When his heart was aching, hers ached as well. When she and Garth looked into each other's eyes and she could see the love reflected there, her love for him surged up inside her the way she knew his love for her was filling him.

And so tonight she knew his loneliness. She

experienced his desperation. Their hearts, their souls, their minds were one. She longed to comfort him, yet knew he was in a place where he couldn't be reached, not even by her.

"Oh, Garth," she said aloud, speaking to the emptiness of the house, "where will all this lead? Will we ever find our way out of the darkness?"

Garth stood at the French doors that lined one wall of the ballroom, gazing out at the blackness of the cold and unforgiving December evening. Tonight a merciless blanket of darkness smothered the earth.

His eyes cast upward, desperately searching, he saw that not even the faintest glimmer of a single star illuminated the sky. The moon was hidden, tucked away behind a thick mass of clouds. Damp air surrounded him, so laden with moisture it was difficult to breathe. Rain approached, another winter storm. And to pave the way for its dramatic arrival, the storm had banished all the light.

Yet the darkness that enveloped Cedar Crest was a mere shadow compared to the darkness that shrouded his soul.

The scene from the night before still haunted him. The image of Corinne's face, twisted into an expression of pure terror, loomed in front of him, indelibly imprinted upon his brain.

She knew.

She had taken one look at him, and something inside her had snapped.

It wasn't rational. Her conscious mind was not what had caused her to react so strongly to the sight of him. On a much deeper level, one far beyond conscious thought, she had recognized the link between the boy sitting on the floor in front of her and the horrific beast that had attacked her under the full moon.

He could not escape his fate. Months earlier, he had fled Portland, desperate to leave the past behind and make a new life for himself. Here, he'd hoped he would be safe. He'd been certain he could . . . if only he could keep himself apart, find refuge in a life of solitude.

Now it was clearer to him than ever than his plan had failed.

Alone at Cedar Crest, Garth's isolation bore down on him, as oppressive as a heavy weight clamped onto his shoulders. Intense loneliness ate away at him, wrenching his stomach, constricting his heart.

Yet through his misery, the terrible agony that tore at him, he felt the pull.

The call of the forest, the enticement of the outdoors . . . of changing into animal form . . .

Tonight the draw was irresistible.

The moon wasn't full. No evil power lurked. There was no imminent danger luring him toward shapeshifting.

This time, it was nothing more than the knowledge that the wolfskin was out there, buried in the clearing . . . that the power to shapeshift was within his grasp.

Never before had he shapeshifted at will. In the past, the change had come about only as the result of the full moon . . . or the presence of such incredible danger that something deep inside him brought about the transformation without him ever making a conscious decision to do so.

He knew it was a mistake. That what he was contemplating was wrong. That being able to transform from man to beast was what had created this private hell in the first place.

But the lure was impossible to ignore. Desperately he wanted to race through the woods, to lose himself in his own power, to forget . . . to escape.

Escape. That was the key. He no longer had any desire to be part of this world. Too many emotions tore at him, too many conflicts ate away at his soul.

Given the choice between being a man and being an animal, he yearned for the simplicity of the latter.

No, he insisted. This time he would refuse to give in. This terrible ability to shapeshift was what he hated most.

It was what made him an outsider.

Garth turned away from the window, determined to forget. Perhaps if he could sleep, seek refuge in obliviousness . . .

He knew, even as the thought ran through his mind, that he would never be able to resist.

As he opened the French doors, a sudden gust of wind rose up, sending a chill through him. He shivered, hesitating. And then he stepped out into the bracing night.

A fine rain had begun to fall. As he crossed over the wall separating Cedar Crest from the wilds, he could hear the drops striking lightly against the rocks and the evergreen needles that carpeted the forest floor. The moist air was fragrant, fresh with the smells of damp bark and wet soil.

He entered the woods, traveling with confidence over the familiar terrain. He hurried to the clearing, the spot where he had buried the wolfskin. When he was certain he'd found the right spot, he dropped to his knees.

Adrenaline pumped through his veins as he began to dig in the soft, moist dirt with his hands. Harder and harder he dug, his movements becoming more frantic. The desire to touch the fur, to feel its softness, to have it surround him, was overwhelming.

And then his fingers made contact with it. The gray hairs jutted out from the dirt. With even greater fervor he plunged his fingers deeper into the dark, rich soil. He was aware that his breathing was so hard and so fast that it sounded almost like panting.

His chest heaving, he struggled to free the huge wolfskin from the blanket of dirt that still half covered it, the coarse granules clinging to the long, thick strands of silvery hair. The rain was falling harder. Garth's hair, now wet, curled around his neck and forehead as he worked. Finally he wrenched the pelt free.

Gathering together all his strength, Garth raised the wolfskin up onto his shoulders. He nearly buckled under the formidable weight. In the end, he prevailed, standing straight and tall in the center of clearing.

The storm had increased in intensity. All around him it poured, great sheets of cascading rain that made it difficult for him to see farther than a few feet.

Yet within seconds his eyesight became sharper. He found himself able to focus on a bush a few hundred feet away, a brook a few hundred yards away. His other senses similarly grew more acute. The smell of the rain, the damp soil, the dried leaves, filled his nostrils. His ears picked up sounds he hadn't been aware of before.

And then, once again, he heard his breath coming more heavily than before. This time, he knew, he was panting, making the sounds of an animal.

The transformation was complete. The werewolf stepped out of the clearing, the spongy soil
giving way beneath his bulk. He moved with confidence, secure in the knowledge that despite the
rain, despite the darkness of the starless night, he
was the most powerful creature in the forest.

As he raced over the uneven terrain, however, he realized that tonight the forest wasn't
where he wanted to be. Instead, he turned
abruptly and began running out of the woods,
toward civilization.

He moved with determination, as if following
a course that had been set out for him by some
other force.

The wolf moved in and out of the shadows,
staying out of view as he made his way through
the streets of the small town. Not another creature was about; instead, silence hung over the
rainy night. The unyielding surface of the concrete felt odd beneath his feet. Harsh colorful
lights assaulted his eyes. This was alien territory,
all hard lines and angles. This, the beast knew,
was a place where he didn't belong.

For a moment, panic gripped him. He had to
get out of here. And then, in the distance, he
heard a terrifying noise: a loud, rumbling
sound, coming closer and closer every second.
Instinctively he hid, leaping into the narrow,
brick-lined passageway between two buildings
and crouching in the shadows.

A screeching sound cut through the night, rubber tires careening over the pavement at a high speed. The wolf recoiled even farther into the darkness. A car whizzed by, moving with reckless speed down the desolate street. He caught sight of three people sitting inside, the driver and two passengers.

And then the car passed under a streetlight. The wolf caught a glimpse of the driver's face.

He reacted with his entire body.

He knew that face. He had seen it before. And the same fear it had elicited before ran through him once again, like a jolt of electricity.

It was a face he associated with fire. A terrible fire, roaring out of control. A fire that devoured a wooden building, greedily swallowed up the trees edging the forest.

The wolf waited until the car had vanished into the night, its red taillights fading as it sped down the street. Then he darted out of the alleyway, once again weaving through the squat buildings of town, this time fleeing what he intuitively knew to be dangerous.

He headed toward a quieter section, where houses lined sedate streets. The rain had lightened up, the drops dancing across the surface of the vast puddles that had quickly formed. The wolf trotted through the maze of streets. His fur was soaked, yet he was indifferent to the rain. Once again he moved over the slick pavement of the road with such determination that nothing could distract him.

Suddenly he stopped. He stood on the side of the street, gazing across at one of the houses on the other side. This, he knew, had been his destination all along. The house was dark except for a single light shining above the front door. He lay in wait beneath a clump of bushes, half shielded from the rain.

Suddenly he pricked up his ears. He'd heard something . . . a car, coming slowly down the street. Without moving, he watched.

A boxy black car pulled up in front of the house. The door swung open and a woman he immediately recognized stepped out.

"Thanks, Bryan," she said. "I had a really nice time tonight."

"I did too," responded the driver. "I'll talk to you soon. And give my love to Miranda."

The werewolf was standing by now, still lurking in the shadows, watching and listening with keen interest.

The woman, he now understood, was his prey.

He stood perfectly still, not a single muscle moving. His eyes followed her as she began making her way across the lawn. She paused after going halfway, opening her purse and rummaging around inside.

The beast had moved out of the shadows. He stood at the edge of the road, still staring at the woman standing near the house, waiting for just the right moment before he darted across the road.

He was aware of a low rumbling sound off in the distance. Something mechanical . . . something menacing. He paid it little heed. He was too intent on his prey. Watching, waiting . . .

And then the time was right. His eyes still fixed on the woman standing helpless and alone a mere hundred feet away, the werewolf leaped across the road.

The next few seconds were a blur. A pair of bright lights, blinding him . . . the piercing shriek of rubber skidding across the wet pavement . . . loud, panicked cries . . . The wolf let out a yelp. He stopped in his tracks, his instincts sending him reeling backward. The car swerved in the opposite direction, its tires slipping against the slick blacktop.

It careened across the lawn, toward the woman.

She let out a scream, her high-pitched cry of terror piercing the rainy night. The headlights shined on her, her arms raised upward, her body frozen to the spot.

The car lurched to a stop, its front fender only a few feet away from her.

The wolf dropped down low, once again hiding beneath the clump of bushes. Terror gripped him, causing his heart to pound furiously. His mind was clouded, his ability to reason somewhere between that of a man and that of an animal, yet still he knew he had come close to meeting with his own demise.

And then the car doors were flung open.

"Mrs. Campbell!" a deep male voice exclaimed. "Are you okay?"

"It was an accident," a second voice, edged with hysteria, insisted. "Honest!"

"I was only doing thirty. I skidded on the wet road when I saw something in the middle of the street. At least, I think I saw something."

The wolf recognized that third voice. It belonged to the driver . . . the one associated with the terrible fire.

"It's all right, boys. Really, I'm fine." The woman sounded shaky, her fear reflected clearly in her voice.

Lights suddenly shone brightly in the windows of the house. A few seconds later, the front door opened. The wolf watched, overcome with a new fear.

Miranda. He watched her come out into the night, seemingly oblivious of the rain. She hurried to the woman's side, her forehead tense.

"Mom! Are you all right?"

"Yes, honey. I'm fine. I just—"

"*You!*" She turned to face the boy who'd been driving. "I should have known you had something to do with this!"

"Hey, I didn't do anything!" The boy held up his hands defensively. "I skidded in the rain, that's all. There was something in the road, an animal or something—"

"An animal?" Miranda's eyes quickly traveled to the road. The wolf burrowed down farther into the wet soil, holding his breath, taking care not to move a single muscle.

"I didn't see anything," one of the other boys insisted.

"Aw, you were in the backseat," said the third. "I saw something, plain as day. It looked like a huge dog or something."

"Yeah, it was pretty big," said the driver. "I'm telling you, Miranda. It was an accident."

"You're not going to call the police, are you?" asked the boy who claimed he hadn't seen anything.

Once again she gazed out in the direction of the road. "No," she finally said. "I guess not."

"Good. As long as you're okay, Mrs. Campbell—"

"I'm all right. At least, I think I am."

The wolf watched as Miranda slung her arm around her mother's shoulders. "Come on inside," she said. "I'll make you a cup of tea. Are you *sure* you're all right?"

The wolf slunk away, his ears flattened in defeat. Inside the massive chest, his heart was breaking. The man was emerging, understand-

ing in a way the werewolf could not. He knew
that tonight he had descended into depths even
lower and more despicable than those he had
been dragged into before.

Turning back to glance at the house one
more time, sorrow stabbed at his heart. Garth
knew now what he had to do.

CHAPTER
10

"Is there anything else I can get for you? Would you like another cup of tea?"

"I'm fine, Miranda. Really. You don't have to wait on me." Mrs. Campbell shrugged her shoulders in a gesture of frustration. "I know you mean well, but it's not necessary for you to hover over me like a mother hen."

Miranda reached across the kitchen table and took her mother's hand. "I'm worried about you, Mom. You almost got hit by a car tonight. That crazy Dave Falco—"

"It wasn't his fault, Miranda. The roads really were slippery. I remember your father commenting on it as we drove back from Norton."

"I still think those boys were driving too fast. Besides, what were they doing out so late, anyway?" Miranda could feel the fury rising up inside her. "That Dave is such a troublemaker. His buddies, Alan and Carl, aren't any better."

"It is possible that his story was true, honey. That he really did swerve to avoid hitting something in the middle of the road."

"You mean that animal he and Alan were talking about?"

Mrs. Campbell nodded.

Miranda could feel the color draining out of her face. "Did you see something?"

A wave of dizziness rose up over her as she was struck by the horrifying realization that it was possible Dave had actually been telling the truth, that there *had* been a large animal in the road. Her stomach lurched at the thought that Garth might have had something to do with the accident that had nearly gotten her mother killed, that he had been at the scene, lurking in the shadows. . . .

"I'm not sure." Her mother thought for a few seconds, her gaze traveling to the window. The faraway look in her eyes told Miranda that she was replaying the terrible scene of a half-hour earlier in her head. "I wasn't paying very close attention. I was too busy rummaging around in my pocketbook, trying to find my keys. It was close to midnight, and I didn't want to wake you by ringing the doorbell. . . ."

"Go on."

"I kept thinking I saw something out of the corner of my eye. A dark shape, moving across the road . . ." Mrs. Campbell shook her head. "It was so difficult to see. The rain, the darkness . . ."

She turned toward her daughter. "I really don't hold them responsible, Miranda. Whether or not Dave really was trying to keep from hitting an animal doesn't matter. I know for a fact that the roads were wet and slippery. I'm convinced the whole thing was an accident.

"Besides," Miranda's mother added, a puzzled expression on her face, "why would anyone want to hurt me?"

He needed her.

Miranda could feel it. The despair she knew Garth was experiencing took hold of her the moment she awoke Sunday morning.

Instantly she was engulfed by a feeling of urgency. Something was calling her, inciting her to react. She imagined she heard a voice, whispering in her ear.

Help him, Miranda. Go to him.

"Garth?" She spoke his name even before she was fully awake.

She rose from her bed, her movements automatic. For a long time she stood in the middle of her room, blinking. The floor was cold and hard against her bare feet. Her white flannel nightgown billowed around her ankles.

"Garth?" she said again.

By now she had shed the last vestiges of

sleep. Her mind was racing as she tried to focus on what was happening.

She looked around her. Her bedroom was covered with oddly shaped shadows, created by the gray light of dawn seeping in through the blinds. Frowning, Miranda studied the furniture that had been hers ever since she was a little girl. She scanned the photographs of her family and her friends that were tacked to the wall, then glanced at her schoolbooks, piled haphazardly on her desk.

Suddenly it all felt so foreign. As if these were the artifacts of someone else's life.

She did not belong here. She was no longer part of this world.

She belonged with Garth.

And then she remembered the events of the night before. Gradually, as she became more awake, the memory dawned on her. The terrible accident . . . or perhaps it hadn't been an accident at all.

So many questions still plagued her. Had there been an animal in the road? If so, was it a bear or something else? Was it possible the animal, whatever it was, had caused the car to swerve, nearly killing her mother, or had something else sent the vehicle veering out of control?

She had to know.

But her first concern was Garth. Quickly she dressed. Miranda took care not to awaken her mother, still asleep down the hall. Moving silently about her room, she pulled on jeans and a thick sweater.

I will go to him, she thought, descending the staircase with the same stealthy movements. I must see him. He needs my help. . . .

Stepping out into the dawn, Miranda braced herself against the chill wind. She glanced up and caught sight of the totem pole towering high above the trees. The head of the wolf was directed toward her, its eyes fixed on hers. Lowering her head, she hurried on her way, through the stark wintry woods toward Cedar Crest.

The forest was silent, an ominous air hovering over Winding Way as she trudged through the new day that was emerging, the sun weakly pushing itself over the horizon, into the pale gray sky. Miranda pulled her jacket more tightly around her. There was something in the air, aside from the cold and the dampness . . . something forbidding.

You're imagining things, she insisted, determinedly continuing along the dirt road. It's just the approach of winter, that's all. Everything will be fine as soon as Garth and I are together again.

And then Cedar Crest came into sight. The mansion suddenly loomed above the zigzagging line made by the pointed tops of the tall evergreens, encircling the house like a barricade. Miranda hoped for a feeling of relief, reassurance from the knowledge that she would soon be at Garth's side. Instead, the mansion's decay, more extreme even than the day before, instilled fear in her.

"Garth?" she called.

There was an edge to her voice as she stepped inside after opening the front door. Had she imagined it, or had it really resisted her pull? Immediately she was struck by the mansion's desolation. Its cavernous rooms felt lonely, as if only sadness dwelled there.

That same fear gripped her as she walked from room to room, her movements slow and uncertain.

"Garth? Garth, are you here?"

Over and over she called his name, her voice pleading. Her heart was pounding. She yearned to see him. Yet at the same time, for a reason she could not explain, she was frightened of what she might find.

Finally she stepped into the garden. How different it was, compared to its freshness of only a few weeks earlier. The stems of the flowers that had bloomed were now brittle and brown, the trees barren. Dead leaves, dry and lifeless, covered the once vibrant place.

At last she found him. Garth sat perched on the edge of an ornate concrete bench, its legs, carved into the shapes of a lion's feet, were crumbling. His face was buried in his hands, his large, strong fingers creating a barrier between him and the rest of the world. His mane of thick blond hair was tousled. His shoulders were hunched, his posture that of a defeated man.

"Garth." This time her voice was a near whisper.

He raised his head, his earnest blue eyes meeting hers. In them she saw a terrible despair, the same sadness that had greeted her when she'd awakened that morning.

She knew then that she had been right to come. He *did* need her. She only hoped that the trials he had endured had not cast him into a place where he would allow no one to touch him.

"You came," Garth said dully.

"Of course I came," Miranda replied.

She stood before him, hovering a few feet away, holding back as if waiting to receive some sign from him that she was welcome here. He gave her no such sign.

"Garth," she said, "I need to know about last night."

"Last night?" he repeated in the same monotone.

"Yes. The accident, with Dave's car . . . were you there?"

"No," he said simply. "I don't know what you're talking about."

"I'm so glad! I was afraid that . . . Oh, it doesn't matter now."

Garth watched impassively as she rushed over to him, kneeling at his feet and grasping both his hands in hers. Her skin felt so soft, so warm. Yet he pulled away.

"What is it, Garth?"

He lowered his eyes. Torment raged inside him, filling him with a self-hatred stronger than any he had ever known.

He hadn't slept all night. The scene from the night before had replayed through his mind, over and over again, until he thought he would go mad.

He had done terrible things in the past. He had committed violent acts. He had killed. Yet nothing he had done before came close to what he had done—what he had tried to do—only hours earlier.

It was unspeakable. Never could he admit to Miranda the atrocity he had been on the verge of carrying out. Even though he knew that the evil power was behind it, even though Miranda would claim to understand, he was convinced she would never again be able to accept him. Not if she knew.

Yet even if he could manage to keep his secret, to go on without her ever finding out, he was certain he would be unable to live with himself. What he had done was too base, too grotesque.

He could not expect her to love him when he harbored only hatred for himself.

Finally he raised his head and looked at her. How beautiful she was! She was like a vision, something too magnificent to be of this world. Her dark hair, thick and full, billowed around her head like a halo, framing her sweet face. Her dark eyes shined with concern . . . with love. She reminded him of an angel, sent down to earth to save him.

Yet instead of finding comfort in her beauty, gazing at her only plunged in deeper the dagger that already cut through his heart.

The time had come for him to do what he knew he must.

"You have to leave," he said flatly.

There, he thought. *It is done.* He tried to ignore the sea of emotions washing over him, feelings that gripped his heart, tore at his soul.

He had tried once before. Sending her away, telling her that theirs was a love that could never be.

In the end, she had come back to him. She had learned what he was . . . and still had chosen to remain.

This time, he knew their separation must be final.

When he forced himself to look at her, he

saw the look of confusion on her face.

"I have to leave?" Miranda repeated the words as if she didn't understand their meaning.

He nodded, a simple gesture that took every bit of strength he possessed. "We can't be together any longer."

"But Garth! I want to stay! I'm determined to help you. I'm not afraid. I still believe that together we can fight this—"

"No. You don't understand." He looked away, no longer able to meet her gaze. His heart was beating at an alarming speed. Every muscle in his body was tense.

He had never dreamed he would lie to Miranda. Yet now he knew he had no choice.

It was the only way he had of protecting her.

"I don't want to be with you anymore."

The expression on her face immediately changed from confusion to shock. As he looked at her and saw the pain he had caused her, something deep inside him died.

"No," she breathed. "I—I don't believe you."

"It's over, Miranda. It's not something I can control. I just . . . the time for us to be together has passed."

She stared at him for a long time. He could see the hurt in her eyes.

"Why?" she demanded. "What happened to change your mind?"

"I can't help what I feel."

"And what *do* you feel?"

He swallowed hard, casting his eyes downward toward the crumbling cobblestones. "Nothing."

She stood up, shrinking back from him. "Look at me, Garth. Look me in the eye and tell me you don't love me anymore."

"Miranda, I—"

"Tell me, Garth!" Her voice was edged with hysteria. "I want to hear you say it. If it's really what you feel, then say it!"

Slowly he lifted his eyes. As they met hers, a jolt of pain ran through him.

Gathering up all his courage, he forced himself to say the words.

"I don't love you, Miranda."

Hearing his own voice pronouncing the words, telling such a grotesque lie, sent a wave of dizziness rushing over him.

No! a voice inside Garth shrieked. *Tell her the truth! Don't cause her such agony! It's a lie . . . a terrible lie. Tell her. Tell her!*

But he knew it had to be this way. The kindest thing he could do was to free her. The curse was too powerful for him to fight. He could not stand by and watch as it dragged her down in the same way it was destroying him. She had to escape while she still had the chance. He had to release her.

He had no choice.

"Now do you believe me?" he asked, his voice hard.

She just stared at him. Already tears were welling up in her eyes.

"Now go. Please. I can't—" Garth's words caught in his throat. No longer could he look at her. He buried his face in his hands, wanting to block out the sight of her . . . wanting to block out everything. At that moment, he wished only that, somehow, he could suddenly cease to exist.

Yet there was no such mercy.

He heard her hurrying away from him, her footsteps growing fainter and fainter. And then, after a few moments, he listened for the heavy slamming of the front door of Cedar Crest.

Garth opened his eyes then. The garden was covered with dark shadows, draped over the withering bushes and the dead flowers like a shroud. He remembered when, for a brief period, this place had been alive. Miranda's love had breathed life into the flowers and the trees, the crumbling stones, even the air itself.

Now the birds no longer sang, the buzzing of the bees had ceased. A stifling heaviness hung over the garden, a feeling of doom that went far beyond the feeling of rotting, of death, that now permeated it.

There was no more life, not for the garden, not for Garth.

Miranda was gone.

It wasn't until she reached home that

Miranda let her tears fall. She raced inside, running up the stairs, glad her mother was still sleeping. Once she reached her room, she threw herself across her bed and gave in to the onslaught of terrible, wrenching sobs.

Never before had she known such sorrow. Her chest ached with it, as if her heart had been set on fire. She was filled with an agony so intense, so focused, it was as if nothing else existed. Every part of her body was filled with despair as she tried to make sense of what had just happened.

I don't love you, Miranda.

The words echoed through her head, a horrific sound that made her want to clamp her hands against her ears. She knew their meaning. How well she understood what Garth was saying to her!

What made no sense to her was the idea of life without Garth. Even attempting to contemplate it caused an emptiness in her that she could barely endure. It was unimaginable, as impossible to picture as life without feeling, life without happiness, life without purpose. She loved him in a way she had never loved before. A feeling that they belonged together, that some force outside them, too great and too mysterious for them ever to comprehend, had always been present. She treasured him, she felt for him . . . she understood him.

At least she'd thought she did. Now she realized she had known nothing. There hadn't been anything in what he'd said or done that had prepared her for this.

Of course, he had sent her away before. But that had been different. He had expected her to reject what he was. He was simply trying to protect her.

Now she knew what he was. And she loved him anyway.

Still, he claimed that her love was no longer enough. And it wasn't. Not if his love for her had died.

Miranda couldn't begin to fathom what had happened. How he had changed, why he had changed . . .

Or perhaps it was that she had changed. She'd been aware from the start that he was distraught over her flirtation with shapeshifting. He had never wanted her to try it, not even that first time when she'd insisted she needed to know more in order to help him lift the curse. When she'd taken it upon herself to change into a werewolf, he had been horrified. His feelings had been reflected even in Cedar Crest, in the way decay had once again crept up over the dignified mansion.

Maybe it was her inability to resist the lure of the evil power that was responsible for his change of heart.

Lying on her bed, unable to summon the will to do anything besides cry, she was certain of only one thing: that what had mattered to her most was suddenly being taken away.

And then, all of a sudden, a new feeling emerged, stubbornly pushing its way into her consciousness. At first she didn't recognize it. And then, slowly, she understood what it was.

Anger.

How can he do this? she thought. How can Garth take something as precious, as wondrous, as unique as our love . . . and throw it away?

He claimed his feelings had changed, yet he had been unable to tell her why. He had said merely that he had no control over the way he felt.

Was it possible she had misjudged him? Had she seen things in Garth that had not in actuality been there? Could his feelings for her have really turned out to be so shallow . . . so transitory?

The anger gathered up momentum, settling in with such intensity that it drove out the despair. Miranda sat up, dabbing at her tears with abrupt movements.

She was energized by this new feeling. The urge to fight back rose up inside her—not against Garth, but against the devastation resulting from his change of heart. There had to be a way to get past this terrible injustice that had been done to her, a way of moving ahead with her life. . . .

Gradually she became aware that the telephone was ringing. Its shrill sound permeated the cloud of anger that surrounded her. Automatically she stood up and went out into the hall, not at all interested in who might be calling, but anxious to quiet the irritating noise.

"Hello?" Her voice was flat.

"Hello, Miranda?"

It took her a moment to recognize the voice at the other end.

"Jeff!" she cried, her tone softening. "What a nice surprise!"

How good it felt to be talking to someone . . . someone who wanted her.

"I hope I'm not calling too early," Jeff went on.

"No, not at all. I've been up for hours."

"Actually, I'm calling on impulse," he went on. "I'm going to be down your way in the middle of the week. I have some business to take care of in a town that's about fifteen minutes away from you. I thought that maybe instead of rushing back to Portland right after, I'd come check out this town of yours."

"Overdrawn?" she teased.

"Overlook," he corrected her with mock seriousness. "You see? This time I remembered."

"I'm impressed."

"I was hoping you'd say that." Jeff paused. "Anyway, I was wondering if you could give me some pointers. You know, fill me in on what hot spots I should make a point of checking out. . . . That is, if there *are* any hot spots."

Miranda laughed. "Overlook's got a lot to offer, but I don't think you'd get much out of visiting it without a tour guide."

"Are you volunteering?"

She hesitated, her mind racing. Why shouldn't she accept a date with Jeff? She no longer had any ties to Garth. He had sent her away, and that meant she was free to do as she pleased.

It took all her strength to ignore the gnawing in her stomach, the aching of her heart. But with a toss of her head, she said, "I'm not doing anything Wednesday after school. I'd love to show you around."

"Really?" Jeff's surprise was reflected in his voice. "Well, then, I'll be there sometime around four o'clock. How does that sound?"

"Four sounds just fine. And Jeff?"

"Yes?"

"Make sure you bring your hiking shoes. The ocean and the cliffs bordering it are beautiful, and I'll make sure you see it all. "But the best parts of the Oregon coast aren't along the shoreline," she told him. "They're in the forests."

CHAPTER
11

Two images loomed in Miranda's mind as she turned the combination on her locker early on Monday morning, so clear they were more real to her than the locker's smooth gray metal surface.

The first was Garth's face, tensed into the same hard expression he'd worn the day before. She could still hear the words that had sent her running away, trying to escape not only him but also the terrible wrenching of her heart, so agonizing it made her dizzy. "I don't love you, Miranda." She longed to forget them, but could not. They were etched too firmly in her memory.

The second image was Jeff's face. She imagined him the way he'd looked coming out of the restaurant the last time she'd been with him, right after the rehearsal in Portland. "When I see something I want," he had told her, "I go after it. And it's only fair to tell you that, when it

comes to you, Miranda Campbell, I don't plan
to give up without a fight."

Conjuring up those two faces, side by side,
Miranda attempted to make sense of the fact
that while she loved one boy, she had made a
date with the other. She tried to picture herself
sharing confidences with Jeff, joking with him,
holding his hand . . . kissing him. Yet every time
she began to focus on one of those scenarios, it
was Garth's face she saw, not Jeff's.

But you have to move on, she told herself
firmly. She slammed her locker door closed,
clutching the books she needed for her first
three classes against her chest. *It's over. You simply have to accept it. Garth made his feelings clear. . . .*

"Hello, Miranda."

She turned at the sound of a familiar voice,
glad for the distraction.

"Hi, Corinne!" she said brightly.

She immediately sensed something was
wrong. Corinne was smiling, but the peculiar
way in which her blue eyes glittered sent a chill
down Miranda's spine.

Then she noticed someone else hovering a
few feet behind: Amy Patterson.

"Just the person we were looking for," said Amy.

"What's up?" Miranda tried to sound casual,
but her apprehension was reflected in her voice.

Even though she was looking at Corinne, it
was Amy who responded. "I heard through the

grapevine that you and Selina have been going around telling everyone who'll listen that you think my idea about lycanthropy being the key to the mysterious attacks is ridiculous."

"Amy, I haven't—"

"It's not as if it's possible to keep a secret in this school," Amy insisted. "I know what you've been doing, Miranda. But it hardly matters. Fortunately, I'm finding out that not everyone is as narrow-minded as you two."

Miranda was tempted to walk away, to refrain from giving Amy the satisfaction of listening to her. But her menacing tone warned her that she'd be better off finding out what Amy had up her sleeve. "I'm afraid I don't understand what you're talking about."

"Don't you?" Amy threw back her head and laughed. "It turns out I've got a supporter for my lycanthropy theory. Somebody else who's not afraid of recognizing that not only is this syndrome real, but that one of our very own neighbors suffers from it."

She paused, pretending to think. "Actually, 'neighbor' probably isn't the best word, as your friend Garth prefers to keep himself as far away from the rest of us as he can get. Living all by himself in a creepy old house, out in the middle of nowhere . . ."

Miranda stared at Amy. "Who besides you would ever believe something so farfetched, Amy?"

Behind her, she heard Corinne say in a quiet, chilling voice, "I believe it, Miranda."

Miranda's head throbbed as she hurried down the corridor to her first-period class. She was overwhelmed by the fact that Amy had finally found a supporter for her dangerous cause . . . and that person was Corinne.

It's such an outrageous idea, she thought as she dashed into Mr. Wexler's classroom just as the bell was ringing. *But is it really possible that Amy could manage to convince the people of Overlook that Garth has lycanthropy?*

And what if they knew the real truth?

It did sound unlikely. Yet Corinne had said it herself. She *did* believe that Garth was lycanthropic . . . and that he was the attacker.

Miranda knew Amy's theory sounded far-fetched. Still, the last thing she wanted was to call attention to Garth—especially if talk about werewolves began circulating around town.

Miranda glanced behind her and saw that Mr. Wexler was in the back of the classroom, explaining something to a student. With a sigh she opened her English notebook, wondering how she was ever going to concentrate on his lecture. Dave Falco suddenly came rushing in. When he spotted her, he stopped.

"Hello, Miranda. How's your mom doing?" he asked, his tone casual.

"She's fine," Miranda replied coldly, barely glancing up at him.

"Hey, you're still blaming me for what happened Saturday night, aren't you? I'm telling you, it wasn't my fault."

"So you've said."

"I'm innocent. Honest!" He held up both his hands, palms outward. "All I did was swerve the car to avoid hitting some stupid animal running across the road."

"That is, assuming this *animal* really existed."

"Believe me, it existed." Dave leaned forward, his palms resting on her desk. His face was right up against hers. "As a matter of fact, it was a big, scary animal. With gleaming blue eyes and pointed ears and long, sharp claws . . . From what I saw, I might even say it was a werewolf."

Miranda drew back. "What did you say?"

"You heard me. A werewolf."

Her mind was reeling. With all the composure she could muster, she said, "Oh, I get it. You've been talking to Amy Patterson."

Dave grinned. "Hey, I'd talk to that babe any time. Especially since she finally dumped McCann. From what I hear, she's in the market for a new man. Who knows? Maybe I'll get lucky this time around."

"Is that why you're buying into her crazy idea about somebody who lives around here believing he's a werewolf?"

Shrugging, he said, "Can't hurt."

"Then I suppose you're also going so far as to pretend to believe it's Garth who's responsible."

"Hey, werewolf or not, I wouldn't be at all surprised if that creepy Garth guy really did turn out to be the nut who's running around Overlook, attacking people." He laughed coldly. "Maybe I'll just come right out and ask him the next time our paths happen to cross. Coincidentally, of course."

"Would you really do such a terrible thing?" Miranda cried. "Would you accuse someone of being a killer simply because of a personal vendetta?"

Dave's dark eyes narrowed. "Hey, all I know is that my pal Mark is still in the hospital with burns all over his gut and a staph infection eating up his blood. He's got so many tubes sticking out of him he looks like something from outer space. And it's all because of what happened that time we paid a friendly little visit to that weird boyfriend of yours."

His eyes still burning into hers, he added, "I swear, Miranda, I was freaked after what happened that night. You pulled some of the weirdest stunts I've ever seen outside of a horror movie."

"So you decided to get even," Miranda returned angrily. "And step one was coming this close to ramming your car into my mother."

"Hey, I'm telling you that wasn't on purpose. Believe me, your mother's not the one I want to get back at."

Miranda just stared at him.

"Besides," Dave went on, his hands clenched into tight fists, "when I finally decide to get my revenge, Miranda, you'll know it."

The two encounters, the first with Amy and Corinne followed so quickly by the second with Dave Falco, left Miranda extremely worried. Even though she was angry and confused over Garth's unexpected change of heart, she still felt loyal to him. Her urge was to protect him, no matter what had happened between them.

If only I could reason with Corinne, she thought, frustrated. To think she and I were once such good friends . . .

When she stood in the cafeteria at the beginning of fifth period, holding her tray and looking for a place to sit, and spotted Corinne sitting alone, she headed right over.

Miranda hesitated at the edge of her table. "Corinne, could I talk to you for a minute?"

Corinne shrugged. "Sure. Why not?"

Gingerly Miranda sat down, pushing her tray out of the way. "I bet you're still not used to being back at school. It's only been a few days. How are you feeling?"

Corinne's eyebrows shot up. "Nice of you to

be concerned, considering that your boyfriend is the one responsible for what happened to me!"

Miranda recoiled. "Corinne, you have no right to go around making accusations like that! Even the police are convinced that your attacker was an animal."

"So I've heard," Corinne returned impatiently. "Funny how their *expert witness* just happens to be your father."

"Are you implying that my father would lie?"

"What do you think? If I were your father and my daughter's boyfriend were going around jumping people in the middle of the night, who knows what I'd do to protect her?"

"But you said yourself you believed him!"

"Only because there didn't seem to be any other explanation. But now—"

"*Now* you've got Amy feeding you crazy ideas."

"Her ideas are not crazy." Corinne sat up straighter. "In fact, her theory about lycanthropy perfectly explains everything that happened."

"It doesn't explain how a human being could manage to inflict wounds on two different people that are identical to those a wolf would have inflicted."

"There you go again, Miranda, expecting everybody to take your father's word."

"If it's good enough for the police—"

"The police are desperate to find an explanation," Corinne said impatiently. "They've got a town full of frightened people on their hands. I heard all about last month's town meeting. Sounds like it got pretty heated, and I'm sure they were only too happy to jump on the first plausible explanation that came along."

Miranda stared at Corinne for a long time. "Maybe I'm not understanding this correctly," she finally said, "but it sounds to me that you're saying you simply don't care about the facts."

"What I care about," Corinne replied, "is what I know in my heart to be true. I know who attacked me, Miranda. And I intend to make sure that, one way or another, justice is served."

As Miranda stood in her living room late Wednesday afternoon, peeking out the front window, she was plagued by nervousness that grew with each passing minute. Yet her tension had nothing to do with the the unsettling encounters she'd had at school earlier in the week. It was almost time for Jeff Jordan to arrive.

She tried telling herself she was blowing things out of proportion. Spending a few hours showing Jeff around Overlook was simply a friendly gesture, she told herself. It was the least she could do, after he'd gone so far out of his way to try to make her feel comfortable in her role as the newest member of the Limelight Theater Company.

Despite her attempts at calming herself, Miranda's heart continued to flutter. She knew perfectly well that she and Jeff were going on a date, not merely nurturing a budding friendship. It was no secret that he was interested in her. He'd made that clear from the very beginning. She had known exactly what she was doing when she had agreed to go out with him.

There's no reason not to go out with him, she told herself, smoothing her hair and checking the light makeup she'd put on in her reflection in the window. *Jeff is kind, funny, and bright. I'll probably have a wonderful time.*

Yet in the back of her mind, she was wondering what Garth was doing tonight. Even more, she longed to know what he was thinking. Did he miss her, too? Did he secretly harbor even the slightest regrets? Or had he walked away from the love they had shared without looking back?

When she saw a sporty red car turn the corner and come down her street, Miranda stepped away from the window. Jeff was here.

She opened the front door as he was coming up the walk. In his hands was a bouquet of flowers, wrapped in stiff paper and tied with a yellow satin ribbon.

"Flowers for m'lady," he greeted her, bowing down low.

"How lovely!" she replied.

"Nothing's too good for my favorite tour

guide." He leaned forward and planted a light kiss on her cheek.

Miranda could feel her cheeks turning pink. Wanting to avert her face, she took the bouquet from him, cradling it in her arms.

"Roses," she murmured. "Yellow roses are my favorite flower."

"I'm glad you like them. I was afraid you were more the wildflower type."

She leaned forward to sniff the sweet fragrance of the delicate blossoms. Yet she found her thoughts drifting. She was remembering another bouquet, a cluster of wildflowers she'd found on her back porch.

"Miranda? Are you all right?"

She gradually became aware of Jeff, lightly touching her arm, his soft words edged with concern. She realized then that tears had formed in her eyes.

"I'm sorry, Jeff. I was just—"

Miranda blinked hard, determined not to let the memory of Garth ruin her evening. She deserved to have a good time. And Jeff deserved her full attention.

"Are you ready for a good workout?" she asked, willing herself to sound enthusiastic.

"What have you got in mind? And please be reasonable. I'm a city boy, don't forget."

"All the more reason to show you the Oregon forest the way it was meant to be seen—on foot. I wasn't kidding when I told you to bring walking shoes."

For close to two hours, Miranda and Jeff tromped through the forest. He started out complaining good-naturedly about the ruggedness of the hike, but soon began asking thoughtful questions. He listened with interest as she told him about the trees and flowers and described the habits of the birds and small animals that inhabited the woods.

She in turn enjoyed showing her favorite spots to someone who was so unfamiliar with this part of Oregon. Looking at them through his eyes renewed her appreciation for the wilds that surrounded her hometown.

"Now I understand why you love this area so much," he told her earnestly as she led him out of the woods, toward home.

"Why, Jeff! Don't tell me a sophisticate like you is turning into a nature lover."

He laughed. "Stranger things have happened."

"Well, I hope that little stroll in the woods helped you work up an appetite," said Miranda. "I know the perfect place for dinner, a quaint little country inn about five miles from here. It's nestled in the foothills, surrounded by the woods with a magnificent view of the ocean—"

"It sounds romantic," Jeff commented. "Let's go."

Miranda and Jeff were seated at a small table

in front of the window. The view was breathtaking, just as she'd promised. The sun had already dipped below the horizon, and the colors of dusk, bright oranges and pinks and lavenders, faded as the dark blue sky of night edged its way in.

The restaurant was nearly empty. An air of intimacy hung over the room, lit only by the bright flames of the fire burning in the stone fireplace and the candles placed on every table.

"How do you like Overlook so far?" Miranda asked after the waiter had taken their order. "I hope you're not disappointed."

"Oh, no," Jeff assured her, his eyes glowing. "If there's one thing I'm not feeling, it's disappointment."

She smiled. "You know, Jeff, the first time I met you, I wasn't sure if I liked you or not."

"Oh, no," he groaned. "What was I doing wrong?"

"You weren't doing anything wrong. It's just that I sometimes get confused by your sense of humor. I'm not sure if you're teasing me or not."

He smiled. "I don't want to confuse you, Miranda. It's true I often confuse myself, but I don't want other people to be affected."

Laughing, she said, "I think I'm starting to get used to it."

"Good," he replied seriously. "I want you to get used to it. I want you to get used to *me*.

Please believe that I'm not teasing when I say I think you're very special."

Miranda could feel her cheeks burning. Suddenly self-conscious, she toyed with the tiny vase of fresh wildflowers on the edge of the table.

"You know," Jeff went on in the same earnest tone, "I'm really glad you finally agreed to go out with me. For a while I thought I was going to have to put up a real fight."

Miranda lowered her eyes. "I probably owe you an explanation. Remember how I told you I was seeing someone else?"

"Of course. What happened?"

She shrugged. "We're not together any-more."

"Well, that poor guy's loss is my gain." He reached across the table and took her hand.

She froze. Her first impulse was to pull her hand back. This felt wrong, all wrong. She didn't belong with Jeff. She belonged with Garth. . . .

Garth doesn't want you! a voice inside screamed. *He doesn't love you!*

"Miranda?" Jeff's voice interrupted her thoughts.

"I'm sorry, Jeff." Gently she moved her hand away. "It's just that—"

"You're still torn up about this guy, aren't you?"

Miranda nodded. "We only broke up a few

days ago. It was entirely unexpected."

"I understand." His voice was soothing. And when she looked into his green eyes, she saw real concern reflected in them.

He was so kind, so attentive. . . . She could feel herself being drawn in by the boy sitting opposite her. The candles on the table cast dramatic shadows across the features of his striking face, enhancing his good looks. His voice was so comforting, so enticing. . . .

Yet she held back. She was trying desperately to put Garth out of her mind, to forget him . . . but she couldn't. He was still there, as much a presence as if he were actually in the room.

"Jeff," she said, "maybe it wasn't a good idea to agree to go out with you, after all. I don't think I'm ready."

"I'm not making any demands on you, Miranda. I want you to feel comfortable with me. I want you to take your time. Don't worry, I can wait. Even if it takes a long, long time."

As he was walking her up to the front door at the end of the evening, Miranded noted that it was a lovely night, the stars providing a canopy of light, the air brisk and fresh. Suddenly she stumbled slightly on a protruding rock. Automatically Jeff reached for her arm.

"Are you all right?"

"I'm fine—"

"Here, let me help you." Still holding her, he walked her the rest of the way.

Why am I resisting? Miranda thought, suddenly so aware of the boy beside her, his hand warm against her arm, his thigh brushing against hers as they started walking once again. *Jeff really cares about me. He wants me. I can't spend the rest of my life mourning a love that has died, wishing for something I've been told I can't have.*

When they reached the front door, Jeff turned to her. He looked at her for a long time, his green eyes locked on hers intently. And then he placed his hands on her shoulders and gently pulled her close. She could feel his breath on her cheek.

"Miranda," he said simply. In those three syllables was a question—a question he was begging her to answer.

She hesitated for only a moment, then raised her lips to meet his.

CHAPTER
12

He had sent Miranda away. She was gone.

Trudging homeward toward Cedar Crest late Wednesday as dusk darkened the winter sky, Garth tried to find comfort in the thought that he'd had to do it. He had no choice. Not if she were going to survive.

Already she had become too much a part of it. Only he could put an end to her involvement. He understood that he was obligated to do it, no matter how great the cost to him.

Now, after what he had just seen, his torment was even greater than before.

And what made it even worse was the knowledge that he alone was responsible for sending Miranda into the arms of another man.

Earlier, looking out at the waning afternoon and enduring a terrible restlessness rooted in his need to forget, Garth had known that he was too anxious to stay inside. Yet venturing into the forest was dangerous. Being there would only augment the pain that tore away at him. Enveloping himself with the glory of nature, returning to the place where the same despicable scene had been replayed so many times, was an abhorrence to him.

Still, the outdoors had called, its sirenlike voice irresistible. Finally Garth turned away from the French doors and left the ballroom. He grabbed his jacket, quickly pulling it on. And then he stepped out into the dying day.

He'd known all along where he was headed. He realized that the moment he felt the fresh, cold air on his face. His destination was as clear to him as the fact that carrying through his mission was bound to break his heart.

He also knew he couldn't resist.

He had to see her. It was true that he was the one who had sent her away. Yet ever since he had, his desire to catch one more glimpse of the young woman he loved, to be near her one more time, was so strong it was a craving—a craving that could not go unsatisfied.

He'd hurried down Winding Way on foot, steering clear of the woods. His strides were powerful and long; even so, his frustration over how slowly he was moving grew with each step. Her face appeared before him like an apparition. While his muscles were becoming fatigued and the coldness of the day nipped at him, he kept on, her lovely features still before him, beckoning to him, urging him onward.

One glimpse, he thought. *Just one more glimpse* . . .

When he reached her house, his heart was pumping furiously. The adrenaline coursing through his body made him agitated, driving him to a nearly intolerable state of anxiety. His desperate need to see her was by that point edged with something else: fear. Fear that he wouldn't see her . . . fear that he would and that his heart would break in two.

He was also afraid he would give in to the urge to run to her, to tell her how wrong he'd been . . . to confess that his insistence that he no longer cared for her was a lie.

Undoing the deed that had already caused him such agony, he knew was the most dangerous possibility of all.

He'd crouched down behind a clump of trees. From there, he could see the front of the house. Through the living-room window, he could see Miranda's mother moving about.

Silently he waited, living for the moment he would catch one more glimpse of her. Her mane of wild curls, the soft, rosy flesh of her cheek. Her knowing eyes, eyes in whose depths he had felt himself growing lost.

The wind had grown sharper, cutting through him like the blades of a hundred knives. Yet as he stood behind a tree, his jacket pulled tightly around him, he didn't care. Still he kept his eyes fixed on her house. The need to see her was growing stronger and stronger until it was an all-consuming desire, one that left no room in his heart for anything else, not even the pain that had held it in its iron grip ever since he'd lied to her in the garden.

I don't love you.

Again and again he could hear his own words echoing through his brain. Mocking him. Torturing him. He shook his head hard, trying to banish that terrible scene from his memory.

Suddenly, he started. A car had driven up in front of the house. Garth watched as a young man he didn't recognize got out, his posture confident, his head held at an arrogant angle.

As he walked toward the front door, he clutched a bouquet in his hand.

The meaning of what he was seeing pierced through Garth, the pain of comprehension so great, so real, it was as if thorns were jabbing at his flesh.

No! a voice shrieked. *This can't be happening!*

Part of him longed to stop it. To run toward the boy who was ambling up the walk toward the Campbells' front door. To run toward Miranda. To explain she was making a mistake, that he hadn't meant what he'd said . . .

And then he spotted her.

Miranda came to the door. She wore jeans and a heavy sweater, a flattering shade of pink that complemented her delicate skin tones. Her hair was a luscious cascade of curls that framed her face. The late-afternoon sun picked up the red highlights in the rich dark color that served as such a dramatic contrast to her creamy skin. Her cheeks were flushed and her dark brown eyes glowed.

Garth's eyes were glued to her as he watched the boy present her with the bouquet, bowing down in a dramatic gesture that made her laugh. Then he leaned forward, kissing her lightly on the cheek.

His heart had contracted with such force that he cried out. Immediately he recoiled, concealing himself in the shadows. *Had they heard him?* he thought, panicking.

Yet part of him longed to be discovered. Perhaps if she saw him hiding in the shadows—watching her, wanting her—she would put an end to this folly. Maybe she would send this boy away, banish him into the darkness of the night. . . .

Her full lips relaxing into a gentle smile, Miranda moved aside to let the other boy in.

Suddenly Garth turned and ran toward the forest. Despite his intentions to avoid what was now a dangerous place, he could no longer resist. He longed to lose himself in the thick growth! To become one with the beauty and purity and simplicity of something so much larger and more significant than himself!

How he craved the chance to snuff out the agony that gripped his very soul!

Racing through the woods, toward home, he was tempted to shapeshift. He hated what he was feeling, yet he couldn't deny the way in which it ate away at him. What a relief it would be to take on the familiar form of a creature of the night. Running entirely on impulse, unencumbered by the impulses of a man. How comforting it would be to retreat to that animal state, one in which he harbored only the simplest of desires: to run free, to hunt, to satiate a hunger centered only in his stomach.

Still, even as he craved the relief that would come from giving in, he knew that what at the moment felt like liberation in reality kept him bound in chains. Shapeshifting, after all, was what had cast him outside Miranda's realm. That ability, to do what few mortals were capable of doing, destined him to a life of loneliness, of torment . . . of separateness.

That curse was what filled him with such self-loathing that he wondered how he would manage to go on.

Still moving slowly up Winding Way, he finally spotted Cedar Crest, its gray facade rising up coldly from the lush green of the evergreens surrounding it. He hurried toward it, desperately seeking the sanctuary it offered. He needed to be alone, apart from the rest of the world . . . cut off from the vision that still haunted him, that of Miranda smiling at the young man standing at her front door.

He stepped inside, expecting to experience the sense of serenity he usually felt coming home.

Instead, he immediately sensed he was not alone.

The evil presence was here. He knew the moment he stepped into the front hallway.

"What do you want?" he cried aloud. Desperately he turned, peering into every corner, scrutinizing each shadow, his arms flailing in what he knew to be a futile search. The silence of the house mocked him.

He knew there would be no answer. What it wanted, it took, without offering any explanations.

Why me?

Garth sank down, the marble cold and hard against his knees. He buried his face in his hands, giving in to the racking sobs he could no longer hold back.

"*Tell me!*" he shouted. "I need to know! Show yourself, whatever you are! You have stolen my life from me! You have destroyed me! At least have the courage to confront me face-to-face!"

The only response was silence.

He fell to the floor, giving in to the despair that had tormented him for so many years, ever since he had turned fifteen and realized his fate.

For the first time in his life, the possibility of not going on felt very real . . . and very much like a welcome relief.

This is it. I've reached the end.

The words came to him suddenly. Yet instead of feeling alarmed, he felt a sense of calm. Of acceptance. Of joy that he had finally come to accept that the burden of the curse was simply too much for one man to handle.

He rose, energized by the conviction that at last he knew what he must do. From deep inside a sense of his own strength poured forth, infusing him with a power unlike anything he'd ever known before.

Garth walked slowly, as if in a trance. Finally he'd accepted his destiny. The final outcome had at last been decided. . . .

And then, suddenly, he felt an odd sensation, unlike anything he'd ever felt before. A thousand hands—gentle, loving hands, the softest he had ever felt—caressed him. Warm, comforting fingers stroked his cheek, his neck, his arms. Instantly they soothed him.

Looking around, he saw nothing.

He knew what they were. And he knew what they were telling him.

Don't despair, their tender touch insisted. *We will help you. We are on your side. We will show you the way.*

The good narnauks. Their power was leading him out of the darkness, back into the light.

Garth's despair vanished. Willingly he gave in to them, allowing them to lead him. Soft fingers encircled his wrists, gently pulling him through Cedar Crest. As he walked, the shadows melted. In their place was a wonderful shining light: warm, enticing, soothing.

They led him to the center of the ballroom. And then, as quickly as they had come, they disappeared.

He was alone.

In the midst of the room, directly in front of him in the middle of the marble floor, was a delicate ceramic figurine, hand-painted in soft pastel shades. A young shepherd, no more than ten or twelve years old, tended two timid lambs. The animals gazed up at him, looking to their protector for safety.

Garth recognized the piece immediately. It was one of the artifacts from the giant wooden crate he'd found stashed in the closet of the room where he slept.

He stood, waiting, staring at the eyes of the figurine. They were a clear shade of blue. In the faint light of the fading day, they appeared almost lifelike. He blinked, not certain of what he was seeing.

Something was happening. Suddenly, all around him, he could feel the room becoming charged with a peculiar energy. Lights darted off the walls, beautiful flashes of red and blue and yellow and orange.

And then, with the same abruptness, his body became infused with the energy. It began at his fingertips, quickly moving up his arms, across his shoulders, and into his chest. He could feel it spreading up and down until it filled his legs, his neck, his head. Within seconds he was suffused with a wondrous power.

In a burst of understanding, he knew. He was about to learn how it had all begun.

"*Show me.*" The words escaped his lips without him having a sense he was about to speak. Yet the demand was suddenly there, hovering in the room, as much a presence as he himself.

A bolt of lightning lit up the ballroom. Within seconds a crack of thunder set the walls trembling.

Garth didn't bother glancing toward the French windows. He knew the storm erupting all around him was not an act of nature. Its roots were in something even more powerful.

And then there was another crack of thunder, this one so loud he involuntarily clasped his hands over his ears and clamped his eyes shut.

When he opened his eyes, moments later, he was no longer in the ballroom.

Instead he was in a forest. Yet he was not in Oregon. He knew immediately he was in a different place . . . and in a different time.

The forest growth was lush. Moist. This was a magnificent forest, untouched and untamed. Thick mosses grew everywhere, creeping up over rocks, edging over the rough bark of trees. A lush carpet of brown mushrooms covered the ground. Here there were no evergreens. In fact, the trees that surrounded him bore little resemblance to those he was used to seeing around Overlook.

As he was studying the woods, so beautiful and yet so alien, he caught sight of a boy. He was young, perhaps eleven or twelve. His clothes were mere rags, tattered and streaked with dirt. He sat on a rock, hunched over.

Garth recognized him as the boy in the figurine.

But the position of his body was different. His face was buried in his hands. Loud sobs wracked his thin body.

Garth's heart lurched. He could feel his desperation. This boy was a stranger, yet he felt a connection with him.

Even though tears streamed down the boy's face, Garth could see the resemblance. There was no doubt he was a Gautier.

Instinctively he knew his name. *Pierre Gautier.*

This boy, this frail, distraught boy hiding in the woods, was his ancestor.

He understood then that he was in France.

And that the boy's garb was so strange because Garth had been transported back in time hundreds of years.

The young boy, Pierre, glanced up. Garth was tense as he watched him glance around nervously. It was clear to him that the child was frightened by the deepening shadows that were slowly overtaking the forest. He jumped at the sound of a hooting owl, the quiet scampering of a small animal hurrying across the forest floor, the whispering of leaves rustled by a sudden gust of wind.

Garth studied his face, streaked with tears. He realized he had seen that face before. The same face . . . transformed into the face of a grown man.

He remembered a vision he had had once before. It had come to him immediately after he'd seen Miranda playing the role of Joan of Arc. When he'd seen her being burned onstage, he'd reacted as if it were really happening.

Later that night the scene had been replayed before him. But the face of Saint Joan had changed, turning into that of a man. A man being burned at the stake.

He understood now that the man in his vision had been Pierre Gautier.

That had been his fate. As a boy, he had been a frightened shepherd. As a man, he had been executed.

The words shouted by the angry crowd came back to him.

"*Tuez-le! Tuez le loup-garou.*"

"Kill him. Kill the werewolf."

It was all snapping into place, the pieces of the puzzle fitting in together. He was finally starting to understand. A wave of relief—of triumph—swept over him. At last, it was coming clear. . . .

All of a sudden Garth froze, his triumphant thoughts coming to an abrupt halt. A loud thundering filled the forest, a noise so overpowering, so terrifying, that any thought at all was impossible.

There was only fear, a terror so strong, so all-encompassing, that it went light-years beyond even the most horrific nightmare, the most dreaded fantasy, the most excruciating memory.

And then he understood. The three horsemen stood before Pierre Gautier. Their clothes were black cloaks, their hoods pulled over their faces. They were large, powerful . . . forbidding. Impatiently their huge steeds pawed the ground, billows of black smoke rising from where they stood.

"Renounce your faith."

The voice of the middle horseman, low and rasping, was familiar to Garth. Even so, it made his blood run cold. The horseman moved forward, his hood falling away from his face. Garth could see that his eyes were nothing more than dark circles, burning as hot and red as coal.

"Renounce your faith," he repeated. "Embrace a new lord, and we will protect you."

Garth's heart stopped beating. For a moment, it felt as if even time itself had stopped. His eyes were fixed on the young boy, standing before the three horsemen. He watched as the tension suddenly left the boy's body.

And then, following a reply in a voice so soft Garth wasn't certain the boy had actually spoken, Pierre Gautier performed one simple motion.

He nodded his head.

"*No!*" Garth's own voice cut through the forest. Once again he shut his eyes, wishing desperately to block out the scene he had just witnessed. He covered his ears with his hands.

"No!" he cried again and again. "No! No! *No!*"

When he opened his eyes, the boy was gone. The forest, the horsemen, the three giant steeds . . . gone.

He was alone. Alone, in the ballroom.

The narnauks were gone. Both the good spirits and the evil spirits had vanished as suddenly and as unexpectedly as they had come. A gust of fresh air swept through the cavernous space, announcing their departure.

The figurine lay in the middle of the floor, in the same spot in which he'd found it.

It had been shattered into a thousand pieces.

Garth knew then that his vision was over.

Yet something still lingered. *Understanding.* Finally, he knew.

The curse of the Gautier family. It had been explained to him. At last, he had seen for himself how it had all begun, how this terrible legacy first came to pass.

A feeling of hope welled up inside him. Hope that, now that he understood the roots of the thing responsible for his torment, he might be one step closer to bringing it to an end.

There was one thing of which he was certain. A new need throbbed inside him, one that would not be quelled.

He had to see Miranda.

CHAPTER
13

Miranda stood in front of the mirror that hung over her dresser, the white fabric of her nightgown billowing around her ankles as she distractedly ran a brush through her hair. She was pensive, ruminating about what a surprising evening it had turned out to be. She reached over to caress one of the yellow roses Jeff had brought, carefully arranged in a crystal vase on top of the dresser. The petals were as soft as silk, and their vibrant color lit up the whole room.

She realized now she hadn't expected to have fun, or even to like Jeff very much. She had only accepted the date with him because she'd been so distraught. Yet she'd truly enjoyed herself. In her head, she replayed moments from their night together. He had been so thoughtful, so sweet, so attentive . . . and kissing him had been lovely.

Yet she still had a terrible aching in her heart.

It should have been Garth! she was thinking as she contemplated her reflection in the mirror. *He's the one I belong with.* Leaning forward to peer at herself more closely, she was struck by the sadness in her dark eyes.

She had tried. Desperately she'd attempted to put him out of her mind. She was angry at the way he'd hurt her. She felt betrayed in a way she'd never felt before. Even her break-up with Bobby hadn't come close to eliciting the kind of heartache she now found herself living with every moment of the day, the sorrow that haunted her even in her dreams.

Even so, she was still having trouble comprehending what it meant.

There was no reason not to believe him. She'd heard Garth say the words himself. He claimed he no longer loved her, that the feelings he'd once had for her were dead.

But imagining life without him was impossible. . . .

Tears welled up in Miranda's eyes. She dropped the brush on the dresser and buried her face in her hands. It was a relief to let the tears fall, just as they had for days, taking her over every time she was alone. There seemed to be no end to them, no limit to the grief that consumed her.

"Garth!" she cried aloud. "Oh, Garth! How could you do this to us? How could you destroy the miracle that you and I created together?"

"Miranda."

She jerked her head up at the sound of a voice, then realized she must have imagined it. Glancing at the clock next to her bed, she saw it was close to eleven. Her mother had already gone to bed. No, she couldn't have heard anything. . . .

"Miranda!"

She hurried to the window, throwing it open. A frigid gust of wintry air burst into the room, whipping through the fabric of her nightgown. Bracing herself against the cold, she leaned out.

"Miranda!" Garth cried, looking up at her from the backyard. "Let me in!"

"Garth! What are you doing here?"

"I have to talk to you. Please, Miranda!"

"Sh-h-h. You'll wake my mother."

"Something's happened."

She hesitated for only a moment. "I'm coming."

As she raced down the stairs, Miranda's heart was pounding. What was Garth doing here? She hadn't expected to see him again. In fact, she'd decided that having to confront him again would simply make no longer being with him even harder. Just seeing his face, looking into his eyes, was bound to elicit such strong feelings that she didn't know if she would be able to tolerate them.

I don't love you. . . .

His words rang through her head, accompanied by all the pain that had been gripping her heart since the moment she'd first heard them.

She grabbed a jacket and threw it over her shoulders before racing through the house, toward the back door. Pausing in the kitchen only long enough to catch her breath, she stepped outside into the night.

"Hello, Garth," she said guardedly. She stood apart from him, resisting the part of herself that longed to throw her arms around his neck and pull him close. As she'd anticipated, just seeing him again caused a wrenching pain in her heart.

He, too, was reserved. He kept his hands thrust deep inside the pockets of his gray suede jacket.

"Thanks for agreeing to talk to me. I was afraid you'd—"

"You said something has happened," she said in a voice that was low and controlled. "It must be important."

"Yes, Miranda. It's very important."

Only then did she look at him closely. In the pale luminescence of the porch light, she could see the look of excitement lighting up his face.

"What is it, Garth? What happened?"

"Oh, Miranda! I saw it! I witnessed the whole thing! It was replayed right before my eyes. . . ."

His excitement was contagious. "What, Garth? What did you see?"

"How it all began."

It took a few moments for the meaning of his words to register. "The curse!" she gasped. "The legacy of the Gautier family!"

Garth nodded. His blue eyes were glowing and his cheeks were flushed. She suddenly realized he was shivering as he stood before her, his jacket a weak defense against the cold of the December night.

"Come inside," she urged, turning toward the house.

He reached for her arm, but deftly Miranda stepped away. Even so, the spot where he'd brushed against her tingled from his touch. Seeing him again, being so close to him, made her light-headed. She had to remind herself to hold back, to keep from feeling what her first instinct was to feel, to refrain from saying the words she longed to say.

She led him into the kitchen, its bright light and enveloping warmth a welcome contrast to the harshness of the outdoors. She sat down opposite him at the kitchen table.

"Tell me," she said. "Tell me everything."

She realized then that his shivering had not been due only to the cold.

"I saw it, Miranda," he began in a voice filled with amazement. There was something else, as well, a different emotion that edged his words. Fear. "The good narnauks led me to the ballroom to show me. They wanted me to see. They knew I needed to understand. . . ."

"Was it another vision?"

Garth nodded. "I traveled to another place. I was in France."

Miranda sat very still. "Go on," she prompted, her curiosity piqued.

"I went back in time, as well. I don't know what year it was. But I could tell it was very long ago. The boy was dressed in tattered clothes, clearly those of another era, probably the fifteenth or sixteenth century."

"The boy?" Puzzled, Miranda shook her head. "What boy, Garth? Who was he?"

"One of my ancestors." He took a deep breath. "Pierre Gautier."

"The man from the vision! The poor soul who was being burned at the stake . . . executed because he was a werewolf!"

"Yes. I already knew what his fate would be, that he was a victim of the family curse. What I didn't know was where his shapeshifting powers had come from."

He took a deep breath before telling her, "Tonight, I saw it for myself. He was alone in the forest, trembling with fear. And then he was approached by three dark horsemen—"

Miranda gasped.

"Yes. Everything was precisely the same as the time you were approached. Except in Pierre Gautier's case, there was one major difference."

"He agreed to trade his soul for special favors."

"Yes. He willingly accepted their evil power in order to win their protection. He agreed to renounce his faith, to accept them—and what they stand for—and their dark lord."

He gripped the edge of the table tightly. His voice was hoarse, so soft that Miranda could barely make out Garth's words. "That was the beginning, Miranda. With a simple nod of his head, with the fear of a young boy who desperately needed help, the Gautier family curse began."

Garth and Miranda were both silent for a long time. Her thoughts were racing, trying to absorb what he had just told her . . . trying to put his desire to share it with her into perspective. She could see both his relief and his anguish. Yet she could also remember the feeling that had gripped her ever since he'd sent her away.

Finally she spoke. "Thank you for coming here to tell me. But I don't understand why—"

"Don't you see, Miranda?" Garth said excitedly. He reached across the table, grabbing hold of both her hands. "We now know all we need to know! The mystery of how the curse came about has been solved! It's the final piece we needed in order to understand, to undo the wrong that's been done, to lift the curse—"

"*We.*" She pronounced the single syllable flatly. "But you and I are no longer a *we.*" There was no judgment in her tone; she simply stated a fact.

"Miranda, please listen to me. I was wrong to do what I did. Ever since I sent you away, I've been in agony. Telling you I no longer love you—"

"You know what you feel, Garth. Only you understand what's in your heart—or what isn't in your heart."

He opened his mouth, as if to speak. But after a moment's hesitation, he simply shook his head.

When he did speak, Garth chose his words carefully. "I need you, Miranda. Fate has decreed that you must be the one to banish the curse; Featherwoman has made that clear from the start. No matter what you now feel for me . . . what we feel for each other . . . you must recognize this."

His blue eyes fixed on hers, he added, "It's your destiny."

Alone at Cedar Crest hours later, standing at the window and watching the dark December night give way to the dawn of a new day, Garth felt a mixture of heartache and hope.

He grieved over the suffering he knew he had caused Miranda, the agony he knew she now lived with every waking moment. How strong the temptation had been to tell her the truth about his feelings for her! How he'd longed to confess! How desperately he'd wanted to declare his love, to explain that his feelings for her had never for a moment wavered . . . that all he wanted was to keep her safe.

Yet in the end, he'd held back. It had to be this way. He could not be with her as long as the evil power controlled his actions.

Still, accompanying that thought was hope. She had agreed to help, even though she believed he no longer loved her. If only the curse could be lifted, if only Miranda could find the way to put an end to the Gautier family legacy . . . if only, if only . . .

The possibility that there was even a chance of resolution was what he lived for.

He tried to imagine what his life would be like without the curse that tormented him, that set him apart from all others . . . that made opening his heart to Miranda, daring to love, dangerous.

Oh, to be free! To be able to experience life the way others did, to enjoy those simple pleasures and complex emotions without fear hanging over him . . . fear of being discovered, fear of causing heartbreak, fear of bringing down with him those people who dared to care about him.

Could his most basic desire ever come true? he wondered, watching the sun floating up slowly from behind the horizon. Was there even the slightest glimmer of hope that he might one day be freed of the horrible curse that had enslaved twenty or more generations of Gautiers?

Garth knew he would find out soon enough. The winter solstice, the time Featherwoman had identifed as the time of the final battle, was now only five days away.

Miranda inhaled sharply, drawing in the brisk early morning air. The forest was at its most peaceful at this hour, when dawn had just broken and the earth felt brand-new. The morning mist, as thick as fog, curled around the stark black tree trunks, wove in and out of the twisted configurations of the leafless branches.

It was a time of stillness, of silence, of serenity. She had come to the woods even before getting ready for school in the hopes that some of that serenity would touch her, quieting the unrest in her heart.

Her mind was racing, as it had through the entire sleepless night. There was so much to think about. Slowly all the pieces were fitting together, the clues that would enable Miranda and Garth to understand how the family curse had evolved in the hopes that they could put an end to it once and for all.

Finally it all made sense. The story of how the Gautiers had come to be cursed hundreds of years earlier, when in medieval France a frightened shepherd, no more than a child, out of desperation entered into an unholy alliance. The tale of how his descendant, Louis Gautier, had come to the New World to seek his fortune as a fur trapper, producing a son he felt he had no choice but to abandon. The saga of that son and the son borne of him, the embodiment of good and evil, fighting an endless battle in the form of two giant werewolves called White Foot and Second One.

Now, finally, Miranda knew the complete history of the Gautier family legacy. At last she understood the curse that had been passed on from generation to generation.

Yet she realized she knew only the beginning.

What about the end? she wondered. *Will this story ever be resolved, or will the curse continue? Will it destroy Garth, the way it has destroyed so many of his ancestors?*

Miranda walked through the woods, stopping when she reached the edge of a cliff. To her right was the forest, thickly covering the sloping terrain, climbing the mountains up to the heavens. To her left, at the bottom of the dramatic drop, was the sea. The waves at Devil's End pounded furiously against the huge boulders jutting out of the murky dark green waters of the ocean.

When she heard a footstep behind her, Miranda started, fear rising up inside her. She turned, searching through the mist to see who approached. When she made out the outline of a small, hunched-over figure emerging through the coils of white smoke, her hands flew to her heart.

"Featherwoman," she cried, relieved. "I didn't expect anyone else to be out so early."

"I had to come." The old woman's voice was soft yet firm. "I had to warn you."

"Warn me?"

"Yes, my child. I was visited by the spirits last night. The spirits came to me to tell me of a great fire. . . ."

The old woman had come up to her by then and was standing only a few feet away. Miranda could see the look of concern on her face, the intensity of her jet-black eyes.

"Featherwoman," she said, "there *was* a fire at Cedar Crest. Weeks ago, at the carriage house. One of the boys who started it was burned—"

"A terrible fire," Featherwoman repeated, going on as if none of Miranda's words had touched her. "It will rage through the night. I saw it. In my vision I saw the flames, reaching upward, high into the sky, swallowing up the night." She closed her eyes. "I felt their anger. I heard their shouts. I heard their words."

"What words?" Miranda demanded, frightened now. "Who was shouting? What did they say?"

The Native American woman threw back her head, her entire body suddenly beginning to shake.

"Featherwoman!" Miranda screamed.

The old woman appeared to be having a convulsion. Miranda stood by helplessly, watching, not knowing what to do.

And then suddenly Featherwoman opened her mouth and the voice of another spoke through her.

"Tuez-le! Tuez le loup-garou!"

And then the old woman opened her eyes. Once again she was calm. She showed no sign of being aware of what had just happened.

"Featherwoman!" Miranda cried. "The voice that just spoke through you . . . who was it? What do they want?"

"They want him dead."

"No!"

"It is their fear that drives them. They want to wipe out all traces. They want to destroy him . . . and they want to destroy Cedar Crest."

"Oh, no!" Miranda buried her face in her hands. "No! Why can't they leave him alone?"

"It is his destiny. But all is not lost, Miranda. Remember: the final battle is near. They are preparing for it. You should be preparing, as well. They will help you. They will show you the way."

Miranda raised her face toward the old woman's. Her words created a glimmer of hope.

"Featherwoman, I had a dream. . . . At least I think it was a dream."

"The narnauks sometimes talk to us while we sleep. They tell us things, show us things. . . ."

"If they were trying to tell me something, I didn't understand it. It was so strange!"

"Tell me about it, my child."

Miranda shook her head slowly as she remembered. "I—I kept stabbing at the air, over and over—"

"Three times."

Jerking her head up, she demanded, "What did you say?"

"Three times." Featherwoman's tone was calm. "In your dream, you stabbed the air three times."

"Yes! How did you know?"

A faraway look had come into the old woman's eyes. "Once near the head, the dwelling place of the mind. The second time in the side, the center of the body."

Her jet-black eyes focused on Miranda. "The third time, in the heart, which houses the soul."

Slowly the meaning of her words dawned on Miranda. "No. Surely you don't mean—"

"You must, Miranda. There is no other way."

"But I can't—"

"You will. For you to follow this course of action has been preordained."

"Stab Garth?" Miranda's voice was mournful. "How could I possibly bring him harm?"

"It is not Garth. It is the evil power. This, you must remember."

"What will I use?"

"You will be shown the way, Miranda. You must have faith. What has been set into motion cannot be stopped."

"Oh, Featherwoman. How will I ever be strong enough?"

"You will be prepared. The good narnauks will show you the way."

"You've told me that before," Miranda cried in exasperation. "But how . . . when . . . ?"

"There is a ceremony. There is much dancing, much feeling. The room is filled with the sound of drums, with shrieks like the sounds of creatures half human, half animal. . . ."

Miranda shivered.

"Do you remember the time I told you about the Big House?" asked Featherwoman.

"Yes," Miranda replied, nodding.

It had been back in October. She'd run into the Native American woman while walking in the forest, and she'd talked about the Oregon coast back when the people of her tribe were the sole inhabitants.

"We built our settlements on the beach, staying near the bays so we would be protected from storms," Featherwoman had told her. "In the center was a Big House, the largest building of the settlement. It was used mainly for ceremonies. We used lime to whitewash it, then painted symbols of animals. Bright colors—red, blue, green—made even brighter by the contrast of bold strokes of black."

Her description had enabled Miranda to picture the building in her mind. Yet she had simply seen the old woman's tale as a fascinating bit of Native American lore. Never had she dreamed that what she was learning about the tribe's past might have something to do with her.

Miranda swallowed hard. "I remember what you told me about the Big House. But I don't understand what it has to do with me."

"It is there you will receive the power. The Big House is where the ceremony will take place."

Miranda's heart pounded. So many questions ran through her mind. Yet she was afraid to ask them . . . afraid of what the answers might be.

"Before the coming of winter," Feather-woman continued, "you must be possessed by the spirit of the wolf. I told you once that the power of the wolf was stronger than that of any other animal."

"How can that happen?"

"It will happen at the ceremony. There they will instill you with the strength you will need to fight the final battle and lift the curse."

"'They?'" Miranda repeated.

"The good narnauks, Miranda. Never underestimate their power." Featherwoman turned toward her, gripping her shoulders hard with her bony fingers. "Never underestimate your *own* power—or the power of your love."

CHAPTER 14

Stepping through the French doors, the gauzy white curtains billowing as a sudden gust of wind rose up, Garth discovered that a bright new day had dawned. The lemon-colored sun struggled valiantly, triumphing against the gray sky to create a glorious day. The crispness of the air felt refreshingly new.

Yet as he stood in the garden, fear gnawed at him.

Five more days. There were only five days left before the winter solstice. Garth found himself anticipating December twenty-first with both dread and hope. The day that Featherwoman had predicted would be the time of the final battle was the shortest day of the year, the official beginning of the bleakest phase of winter. . . .

And the night of a full moon.

He would shapeshift that night, he knew,

watch helplessly as his body went through the bizarre changes that converted him into a wild beast. The evil power would take over, controlling his actions, willing the animal to do things that were inconceivable to the man. . . .

Yet despite his apprehension, another thought, a hopeful one, hovered in his mind: If Featherwoman's prediction turned out to be correct, the night of the winter solstice would be the last time he would ever shapeshift.

How he longed for her words to come true! Yet there were still so many things he and Miranda didn't know. The pieces of the Gautier family history finally fit together . . . but it wasn't enough. They needed to know about the ceremony itself, the ritual she would have to perform. . . .

The possibility of failing—of either being forced to live on in this way for the rest of his days, or of perhaps sinking even further into evil—was one he dared not even contemplate.

If only I could figure out what we still need to know! Garth thought. He remembered back to the day he and Miranda had visited Featherwoman at her cottage, nestled in an isolated section of the forest. She had shown them a rolled-up piece of parchment. The drawings on it told the tale of Second One and White Foot. There were also three lines, signifying the three things that were required to fight the evil power.

"You will know when the time is right," she had told them.

Now the time was drawing near. Suddenly overcome with hopelessness, the fear that the questions still haunting them would never be answered, Garth sank onto the crumbling stone bench.

"When will we know?" he cried. "The time is growing close. Soon the winter solstice will be upon us, and we must be prepared. Yet there is still the question of what we will need to fight the final battle—"

Desperation gripped him as he sat his with shoulders hunched over and his face hidden in his hands. He was certain, at that moment, that there would never be an end to the curse.

Suddenly he felt gentle fingers grasping his wrist and lifting his hands away from his face. Their touch was so soothing that he did not resist. Blinking at the brightness of the day, he looked around. He knew who had approached him. Yet he didn't know why. . . .

And then he spotted it, on the bench next to him. The jewel case from the cache of treasures he'd found stored in the closet in his bedroom. The small box fit in the palm of his hand. Made of wood, it was painted a delicate shade of pink and trimmed with gold leaf.

A design was hand-carved onto the lid. Garth had noticed it before, yet had never taken the time to study it. This time, as he held it up to his face, every detail was illuminated by the bright morning sun. Carefully he examined the pattern.

It consisted of swirling lines, intricate curlicues playing off one another to form a pleasing image. Garth held it cupped in his hands, staring at it, mesmerized. As he did, the jewel box grew warm.

He did not put it down. Instead he kept his eyes fixed on the complex design on the lid.

Before long he found himself unable to look away.

And then, slowly, the image began to change.

The swirls moved slowly at first, drifting across the top of the jewel case with a motion so subtle it was almost impossible to detect. They moved faster and faster as he watched, fascinated, his excitement growing.

The lines formed a curve, almost a perfect oval shape that covered the entire top of the box. Other lines filled in the details: shadowy areas that looked like eyes, a twisting line that resembled a mouth stretched into an angry grimace. Along the top were strange shapes, sticking out at odd angles. Finally they became clear enough for Garth to make out what they were: feathers, twigs, bits of bark. . . .

And then he realized what he was seeing. A chill ran down his spine.

The tribal mask. The Native American artifact he'd found stashed in the closet at Cedar Crest.

The image remained for only a few moments. Already the pattern was reforming, the lines that had created the first image rearranging to form a second.

This time, the picture was more intricate. The heads of several different animals appeared, scattered in a random pattern. An eagle, a frog, an owl, a whale . . . and finally, a wolf, all of them looped together by a wavy line.

He knew he had seen this image before. Yet it took Garth a few seconds before he could place it.

The memory came to him in a sudden flash. The necklace. Miranda's necklace, the one she'd worn the night of the Homecoming Dance and at her Christmas party.

And then the lines began moving once again. The animal heads on the cover of the box melted. Instead, two straight lines formed, joining together at one end. At the other was a T-shape. The outline of a single object, simple and easy to make out, was laid out before him.

A knife.

It was not just any knife, Garth knew. It was the knife Miranda had told him about, the one she'd found at that peculiar shop in Norton. She'd hidden it in a cardboard carton at the bottom of her closet . . . and it had vanished.

Three different images. The tribal mask, the necklace, and the knife. But what did it all mean? Why were three such different objects being shown to him?

Garth's eyes remained fixed on the jewel case. Anxiously he waited, curious about whether more images would be shown to him. Yet this time, when the lines once again began their peculiar dance, they recreated their original design.

Three different images, he thought, confused, putting the box down in frustration. He repeated the names of the objects over and over in his mind. The mask, the necklace, and the knife. Three things, shown to him by the narnauks, presented to him in a manner that made it clear they wanted him to take notice. . . .

And then the hair of the back of his neck rose. Suddenly he understood.

Featherwoman's words echoed through his head. "You will know when the time is right."

Now he knew. The time was right. At last the final piece of information, the last clue, had been revealed to him.

The narnauks had shown him the three items necessary for the ceremony, the three things Miranda would need to fight the final battle.

"Miranda!" he cried, rising up from the stone bench and lifting his arms upward, toward the heavens.

*   *   *

Garth ran most of the way to Miranda's
house. The sun was rising higher and higher in
the sky, driving away the last traces of white mist
that still lingered in the forest. Yet already
clouds were moving in from the west, heavy with
moisture from the sea. The brightness of the
winter day was soon going to fade, the delicate
pastels destined to succumb to the bleak shades
of gray.

When he reached her house, he pounded on
the front door.

"Miranda!" he called, his voice edged with
desperation. "Miranda, I have to talk to you!"

When Mrs. Campbell opened the door, she
looked puzzled.

"Garth, are you all right?"

"I have to see Miranda. Where is she?"

"She's at school. If you'd like, I could tell her
you came by—"

He was already sprinting away, toward the
low brick building. He knew the way, yet as he
neared it he slowed his pace. He'd never ventured inside before, thinking of it as a dangerous place. Inside were people who feared him . . .
people who hated him.

Yet he had to see her. The clock was ticking,
the day of reckoning growing closer. If he and
Miranda were going to join forces to see through
to the end what he'd come to believe was their

destiny, he had to set aside his own fears.

It was the only way.

The school building felt alien to him. Scuffed linoleum floors, drab cinder-block walls lined with metal lockers, sharp angles and harsh lights . . . for a few moments, his instincts told him to retreat. He didn't belong in this place. He was tempted to turn and flee. . . .

Miranda. I must find Miranda.

He raced through the corridors. Before long the shrill sound of a bell cut through the silence, and almost instantly the halls were crowded with students. Garth blinked, recoiling. Only one thought held him there: *Miranda.*

He stood at the end of a corridor, completely at a loss as to how to find her, when suddenly he felt someone slap him hard on the back.

"Well, look who's here." Dave Falco stood before him, a smug smile on his lips and a hard glint in his eyes. Amy Patterson leaned against him. Their arms were slung around each other's waist. "Hey, Garth, I was thinking about you just the other night. There I was at the video store, and all of a sudden I saw this movie called *I Was a Teenage Werewolf.*"

Amy laughed flirtatiously. "Oh, Dave. You're such a riot!"

"See that?" He glanced over at her, clearly pleased by her reaction. "I've got other talents you have yet to discover."

"I'm looking for Miranda." Garth struggled to keep his voice even. Inside the pockets of his gray suede jacket, his hands were clenched into fists.

"Of course you are," Amy said. "Why else would you be here?"

"Maybe he's shopping for his next victim," Dave quipped.

Amy tossed her mane of long blond hair, then pulled it over one shoulder. "Or maybe you should say his next *prey.*"

Anger rose up inside Garth. He understood better than ever what Miranda had been dealing with nearly every day since she'd pledged her love for him. And he wanted more than ever to protect her.

How tempting it was simply to leave town, to disappear from her life forever! Perhaps then the evil force would stay away from her. Maybe that was a way to disentangle her from the horrible web into which she'd been drawn. . . .

Yet Featherwoman had claimed fighting the final battle was her destiny. The choice had been made for them. He had to stay . . . and Miranda had to fight.

Together, they had to triumph.

There would be no rest until then. There was no decision to make, no other course even to consider following.

Following this path was what fate had decreed.

"You know what I think, Amy?" Dave went on. "I think our friend's days as a hunter are numbered." He fixed his dark eyes on Garth. "It's a funny thing about us small-town folks. We're not crazy about strangers coming in from the big city and clawing us locals to death. Or performing magic tricks that can't be explained—especially those involving fire."

"Look," Garth said, no longer able to keep the impatience out of his voice, "all I want is to find Miranda. Can either of you tell me where she is?"

"I'm sorry I don't keep closer track of her whereabouts," said Amy. "But I can tell you one thing. She's guaranteed to put in an appearance at the town meeting tonight. Andy Swensen's mother is leading a movement to keep Overlook from doing its usual Christmas thing until the mystery of the night stalker's been solved. There happen to be a lot of very angry people in this town, and I'm sure your feisty little girlfriend can't wait to take them on.

"In fact," she added, a cold smile playing at her lips, "it might not be a bad idea for you to come along too. After all, there's a *slight* possibility your name might come up."

"Or maybe a little more than slight," Dave said, grinning. "You're becoming more and more popular every day, Garth, my boy. I'm sure there are a lot of people around here who'd jump at the chance to get to know you better."

"Unless you've already got other plans," Amy said. "Wait a minute—is there a full moon tonight?"

Garth turned away. He strode down the hall, his ears burning at the sound of Dave and Amy laughing loudly.

He found her in the school library, sitting cross-legged on the floor, studying the book lying open in her lap.

"Miranda!" he cried, bursting through the double doors. "I was afraid I'd never find you!"

"Garth, what are you doing here?" Miranda scrambled to her feet. "Are you all right? What's happened?"

"I—I have to talk to you. I know the three things we need to undo the curse—"

Miranda placed her hand on his arm. Looking around the library, she told him, "Let's go somewhere we can talk. There's a small study room in back."

Once they were alone, her face lit up excitedly. "Tell me, Garth. What happened?"

"Miranda, I had another vision."

She gripped him by the shoulders. "What did you see?"

"It wasn't like the other times." He glanced toward the door, checking to make sure it was closed. "This time I saw the images on the cover of the jewel case I'd found stored in the closet at Cedar Crest. Here."

He reached into his pocket, gently pulling out the pink and gold jewel case. Holding it with a sort of reverence, he presented it to her.

"The swirls on the lid," he said, watching as she carefully cradled the small box in the palms of her hands. "They changed shape. They took on new forms." He paused before adding, "They showed me things."

"What things, Garth?"

He took a deep breath. "Do you remember the words of Featherwoman? Do you remember what she told us the time we went to her cottage in the woods, seeking answers to our questions?"

Miranda nodded. "Of course."

"She said there were three things we would need to undo the curse of the Gautier family."

"She didn't tell us what they were," Miranda recalled. "She said we would know when the time was right."

"That time is drawing near." Garth looked down at the box, the vision he had had replaying in his mind. "I saw them, Miranda. I saw the three things. The good narnauks showed them to me, using this box as their medium."

Miranda grew pale. "What are they?"

"The Native American tribal mask that was also stored in the crate is the first."

Miranda nodded. "Yes," she said. "I remember it. I saw it at Cedar Crest."

"The second was the necklace."

"My necklace?" Automatically Miranda raised her hand to her throat.

"Yes. The one with the animal carvings. The one with the wolf."

"I understand now," she said. "I've already experienced some of its powers." She was growing more excited. "We have these things, Garth. They're ours."

Garth held up his hand. "The third one . . ." Anxiously he searched Miranda's face, afraid of what he would see there. "The third was the knife."

As he expected, her expression grew stricken.

"The knife," she repeated, her voice hoarse. "But it's gone! The old mountain man said he'd seen it in a stream. . . ."

He simply nodded. "We have to find it."

"But how—?"

"Featherwoman told us we would know, when the time was right. She said the good narnauks are on our side."

"Yes, but how . . . ?"

"I've learned that it's not our place to ask," said Garth, his voice soothing yet filled with confidence. "The good narnauks have shown us the path so far. I no longer fear that they'll abandon us, Miranda. I believe they will show us the way. Remember, Miranda, we must have faith."

He glanced down at her and saw she was gazing up at him with trust in her eyes.

He hesitated, the unspoken words hanging in the air between them. In the past, whenever they had spoken of their faith, they had also spoken of their love, trusting that the depth of their feelings for each other would see them through the ordeal ahead. Now there was no more talk of love.

He gazed at her, longing to hold her but knowing he could not. Garth wondered how Miranda could look into his eyes and not feel how much he loved her.

But he remained silent. One day, perhaps even soon, he would tell her of his love, confess that it had never for a moment wavered. But this was not the time.

He only hoped that, somehow, he would know when the time was right.

I have to find the knife, Miranda thought, riding her bicycle as fast as she could along the main road that connected Overlook with Norton.

All day, since Garth sought her out at the school library and told her about his vision, apprehension had gnawed away at her. It was true she had faith that, in the end, the good narnauks would help them prevail. Yet there was still so much to do. The winter solstice was growing near, and she had to be prepared for the final battle. And then what if they didn't prevail? What if the dark side won? Then where would she and Garth be?

It was imperative that she recover the knife before it was too late. . . .

She rode down Moss Avenue, barely glancing at the shops that usually brought her into Norton. Instead, she headed toward the far end of town. It was there, on a tiny side street, one she'd never before paid much attention to, that she'd stumbled across the shop in which she'd bought the knife.

ET CETERA, the sign nailed over the front had read. Underneath, in smaller letters, were the words, "Oddities, Antiquities, and Other Glorious Junque."

As she slowed down to pass a line of parked cars, Miranda thought back to the day she had first seen the knife in the glass display case at the rear of the shop. Desperately she searched her memory, trying to remember something, anything, that would help her figure out how to get it back.

She hoped that returning to the shop would provide her with some clues. It was a long shot, she knew, but she wanted to try to find out more. Perhaps the old man who ran the curious little store knew something about the knife, an important detail he'd neglected to mention. Or maybe if she pressed him he'd be able to remember how it had first come into his possession. Who had brought it . . . why the person who'd sold it to him had wanted to be rid of it.

Or perhaps, she now realized, it hadn't been a person at all that had enabled the knife to find its way into the shop . . . into her hands.

She was desperate to find the knife. And if there was any way she could find even the tiniest shred of information, anything at all that would help her locate it, she would do her best to pursue it.

And so her heart was pounding as she neared the corner, the place where she'd first seen the sign advertising the shop. A poster had been tacked to a telephone pole. "Looking for the unusual?" it had read, with an arrow underneath.

The poster was gone, she noted as she got near. But that didn't trouble her. It had probably been torn down, she reasoned. Or perhaps it had been blown away by the wind.

She turned the corner then, stepping hard on the brakes of her bicycle. Already the questions she wanted to ask the shop's proprietor were forming in her mind. Adrenaline pumped through her body as she anticipated the possibility of finding out something—anything—that would aid her in her quest.

Eagerly she scanned the storefronts lining the block. She frowned, not seeing it. She remembered it so clearly, the narrow shop with its doorway set back from the sidewalk five or six feet. The faded sign, in poor condition, had been easy to spot.

Yet as hard as she searched, she didn't see it.

Slowly the realization came over her, a tingling feeling that traveled down her body as she stood with her bike, studying the facades of the shops.

It was gone.

"Did I imagine it?" she whispered, tightly clutching the handles of her bicycle. "Was I dreaming? Did any of it happen at all?"

There were no answers to her questions. There was only the stillness of the late December afternoon, unbroken by even the sound of a single bird chirping.

CHAPTER
15

Garth stood outside the Overlook Grocery late Thursday afternoon, watching the comings and goings of the people who lived in town. They went in and out of the post office, stopped at the bank, came out of the grocery store carrying bundles. Some of them hurried, running their errands with a sort of earnest resignation. Others appeared to enjoy the everyday routine of small-town life, chatting with the neighbors they encountered, lingering to study a window display, taking the time to read a poster tacked to a telephone pole.

He envied each and every one of them. As he watched, Garth was jealous of the fact that they were all ordinary people. He realized they had problems. Yet compared to him, they were wonderfully unencumbered. Not one of them had even come close to experiencing anything of the magnitude of what he contended with every single day of his life.

He knew that, tonight, a meeting was being held to discuss whether or not the town of Overlook should go ahead with its usual holiday festivities. So many people saw this as a dark time, one in which a celebration of any kind was distasteful. And, as he knew only too well, the attacks that he himself had perpetrated were the reason for the controversy.

He had to live with this knowledge, this agony, every hour of every day. The most formidable challenge in his life was finding a way to cope with the reality of what he was . . . and what he had done.

Walking home, cutting through the small parking lot between the bank and the post office, Garth's heart was heavy. Even so, he could imagine the kind of serenity these people experienced. How he craved it! How he longed to live a life like theirs! To be free of the curse that had tormented him for so long . . . that alone, he was convinced, would be enough to ensure him happiness for the rest of his days.

Trudging up Winding Way through the approaching darkness of night, the magnificent house looming up ahead felt more like his prison than his home. Another evening of solitude lay ahead of him, another long night of anguish as he lamented the hand that fate had dealt him.

Garth went into the library, a small room that had on occasion provided him with some solace. In here, surrounded by books, he didn't feel quite as alone. In their pages were voices, the thoughts and feelings of other people who reached out to him, wanting to touch him, wanting to talk with him.

Yet even in this room, a terrible restlessness nagged at him. He desperately needed a distraction. He lit the fireplace, immediately feeling comforted by the fire's bright light and its welcome warmth. Then he turned to the wooden bookshelves that lined three of the room's four walls, running from the floor all the way up to the ceiling.

Next he lit a candle, holding it up so he could read the titles on the rows of books before him. It was difficult, making out the gold lettering embossed on the volumes bound in fine-grain leather, deep red and brown and forest green. Not only was the darkness of the room an obstacle; the entire collection was coated with dust. Repeatedly he ran his fingers over their bindings, needing to clear away the thick layer of gray before he was able to make out the titles.

He recognized most of them. These were the well-loved classics that had traveled through time, stories that lived well past their creators: *Moby Dick, Doctor Jekyll and Mr. Hyde, Crime and Punishment* . . .

And then one volume in particular caught his eye. It looked different from the others: taller, slimmer, its dark blue binding more worn. Something else made it distinctive, as well: no title was printed along the spine.

Curious, Garth reached up and pulled it off the shelf. Holding the candle up against the front of the book, he saw that the words printed on the cover were obscured by a thick layer of dust. With his hand he wiped it clean.

The Autobiography of a Tortured Soul, the title read.

Without a moment's hesitation, he hurried over to the fireplace, where he hoped there would be enough light to read the small print. Kneeling down on the hearth, holding the slim volume close to the crackling flames, he opened it.

Inside the cover, the title was printed once again. Below it were the words, "Written and published by Claude Gautier."

Garth let out a cry. Claude Gautier was his great-grandfather, the man who had made his fortune in the lumber industry at the beginning of the century . . . the man who had built Cedar Crest.

With shaking fingers he turned the page. His eyes immediately locked into a pair of eyes in a photograph printed on the frontispiece. They looked so much like his own eyes that he gasped.

Once he got over his initial shock, Garth

studied the photograph more carefully. It was black and white, the look of it that of a much earlier era. A date was written underneath: 1928.

The man in the picture looked as if he were in his late thirties. His hair, thick and curly and light-colored, was cut short in what Garth surmised was the style of that time. He wore a mustache and a pair of wire-rimmed glasses, two perfect circles balanced carefully on his nose. The features of his face were strikingly handsome. His nose was straight, his chin square and strong, his blond eyebrows bushy.

The resemblance between Claude Gautier and Garth was remarkable.

While the man in the photograph wore a stern expression, the look in his eyes warmed Garth. This was a man who had struggled during his life, he sensed, learning as much about kindness and compassion as about the harder, uglier aspects of a man's existence. He saw sorrow there, as well. He had clearly suffered a great deal during his four decades, perhaps even more than most other men his age.

Immediately Garth felt a strong kinship with this man, a connection that transcended the many decades that separated the two of them. Standing here, in the very house this man had built, the place that had represented his reward for having found monumental success at an impressively early age, he felt as if he actually knew him.

Even so, Garth was filled with trepidation as he turned the page one more time.

The following page was headed with the words, "My Story." His heart pounding, Garth began to read.

"For years I have pondered the question of whether or not to record my story," the book began. "I have won some success in my life; some might say I have achieved greatness. Born of humble beginnings, the son of a merchant with little formal education and few opportunities to make his mark on the world, I built an empire. From out of the Oregon woods I created a flourishing lumber business, realizing the vision I had had as a young man.

"During my lifetime, I have also achieved personal fulfillment," the memoirs of Claude Gautier went on. "At the age of twenty-one I married the woman I had loved for three years, a woman with a face as beautiful as the most precious flower and a spirit as pure as an angel's. Since the first time I laid eyes on her, I loved Elizabeth, barely daring to hope that one day she would consent to be my wife.

"Together she and I produced a perfect child. The birth of our son was the happiest moment of my life. How I loved my family! Elizabeth and Henri were everything to me.

"And there were more riches in store for me. The lumber business that I began as a young man quickly blossomed. By the age of thirty I had made my fortune. And so I built what I was convinced was my just reward.

"I created a French castle, looking back to my family's roots I had traced in my youth to France . . . and looking ahead to the future generations of Gautiers, whom I hoped would one day benefit from my prosperity. Here in the wilds of Oregon, with the powerful sea crashing on one side and the magnificent Cascade Mountains on the other, I built a palace.

"I named it Cedar Crest. The word 'cedar' comes from those fine evergreens that allowed me to build my personal fortune. The word 'crest' refers to the ridge on which the mansion was built, but I also chose it because crest means the highest or the best. This house—my home—represented the culmination of everything I had ever worked for.

"To live in a place as magnificent as Cedar Crest with my wife, Elizabeth, and my son, Henri, was the realization of a lifelong dream. I saw myself as the king in a children's storybook, privileged enough to live happily ever after.

"Yet in the end, that dream turned out to be nothing more than a nightmare."

Garth paused in his reading, raising his eyes and staring into the fire. He no longer felt the fear he'd experienced when he'd first opened the book. Instead, he felt a heaviness, a sadness, that bore down on his soul.

Claude Gautier's story, he realized, closely paralleled his own.

Garth, too, dreamed of such a life, one characterized by prosperity, to be sure, but more important, one filled with love. He had seen Miranda when he was the exact same age that his great-grandfather had been when he first laid eyes on Elizabeth, the woman who three years later was to become his bride. Like Garth, Claude Gautier had fallen in love immediately, seeing in one particular woman a remarkable purity of mind and spirit, recognizing the uniqueness of such an individual . . . and comprehending how valuable and how special it was.

Garth reflected on the fact that he had never been told the complete story of his great-grandfather's life—or that of any of his other relatives. He remembered hearing snatches of conversation as a child, bits and pieces that told him the man called Claude Gautier had led a tragic life. But the details had eluded him—up until now.

Determined to learn the truth once and for all, he turned back to the book, straining to read the rows of small print illuminated only by the fire's flickering orange-red glow. For hours, Garth read. Again and again he piled more logs into the fireplace, needing not only its light but also its warmth. With great eagerness he drank in the details of his great-grandfather's life. Repeatedly he was struck by the parallels—in their experiences, but also in their feelings.

He read about the first time Claude Gautier had shapeshifted. Just like Garth, it had been when he was fifteen years old. The book went on to describe many more episodes, changing into a wolf under the full moon. Eventually his great-grandfather was transformed into a beast on other occasions, as well, sometimes as a result of his own will or actions, other times spontaneously, the change initiated by the evil power. His heart ached for the man as he read on, each scene playing through his mind so clearly it was as if the other's experience were his own.

What was even more painful, however, was reading about the destruction of what was once a close-knit and loving family. Elizabeth tried desperately to accept what he was, but in the end could not. She returned to her parents, a broken woman.

As for Henri, he, too, began to shapeshift at the age of fifteen. Once he understood the family legacy, he cursed his very birth, blaming his father for creating what he himself pronounced a monster. He ran away from home, cutting off contact with both his parents, so angry he wanted nothing more than the chance to forget his past. Claude, like Garth, recognized that

Henri's wish was an impossibility. There *was* no forgetting . . . no escaping.

It was close to midnight by the time he reached the book's end. The fire was beginning to die, and there were no more logs stacked up in the library. Garth experienced no fatigue. With the same eagerness with which he had begun, he devoured the words, perusing page after page. Yet that same sorrow overwhelmed him as he read the concluding paragraphs of his great-grandfather's memoirs.

"Now they are gone," Claude Gautier had written, no doubt feeling the same sadness that Garth felt upon reading his words. "Everything I have ever truly cared about has vanished like the morning mist rising off the forest. And as I sit here all alone at Cedar Crest, looking back, I realize this is how my story had to end. For how else could I have expected my wife and my son to act? Elizabeth loved me, but even she, with her pure and giving heart, could not be expected to love a murderous heart. Henri, as well. Early on, he came to learn that inheriting the Gautier family name meant living with a legacy of torment. Of rage. And above all of loneliness.

"Now Cedar Crest haunts me. Its very beauty seems to mock me. With all its elegance, it cannot begin to make me happy. Only one thing could accomplish that: to banish this wretched curse forever!"

There were tears in Garth's eyes as he closed the book. How well he understood his great-grandfather's experiences! How closely he identified with the torment he had felt!

Seeing for himself the torturous life the man had led made Garth feel his own loneliness and sorrow that much more strongly.

Reaching up toward the shelf, he was overwhelmed by the seeming inevitability of the Gautier family curse. He was more convinced than ever that he was destined to live the same life of tragedy that his great-grandfather had lived—and his great-grandfather before him, and his before him. Why should Garth dare to believe he could ever free himself of this wretched curse that had plagued generation after generation of Gautiers?

As he was about to slip the book back onto the shelf, something caught his eye. It was tucked behind the other books, partially concealed. Reaching in, Garth retrieved a square of carefully folded cream-colored paper. It had clearly lain pushed behind the books for decades.

Puzzled, Garth unfolded the thick paper. It was fine stationery, he saw, embossed at the top with two elegant golden letters: E.G.

"My dearest Henri," the letter began, the words written in ink in a flowery script. "I know you requested long ago that you and I cease to be in communication—a request that would of course break any mother's heart, just as it did mine. And up until this point, I have striven to honor that request, recognizing that as a grown man, you have a right to make such choices. But there are special circumstances that compel me to write to you."

With that same feeling of foreboding that had haunted him for much of the night, Garth read on. He was eager to know what his great-grandmother had written in this letter to her son, yet at the same time he dreaded it.

"It is with the greatest sadness that I inform you, dearest Henri, that your father died three nights ago." The letter went on to express the grief that gripped her, even though she herself had not seen Claude Gautier for years. Garth scanned the words of sadness, a witness to a widow's pain, yet still searching as he tried to find out what had caused his great-grandfather's death.

It wasn't until the end of the letter that his question was answered.

"In closing, my son, I will say I regret that I cannot tell you the most obvious of facts: what was responsible for your father's death. I do know that he went into the woods three nights ago. The Power was present. This, I found out from the townspeople living near Cedar Crest. They reported that there was a terrible wind-storm that night. The sea was in a rage, the giant waves crashing against the boulders at Devil's End with a fury greater than ever before. The sky was alive with lightning and thunder, terrible flashes of fire cutting through the black sky, loud rumbles so deep and so powerful that they caused the earth itself to tremble.

"And of course there was a full moon. We both understand the significance of that fact—only too well."

Garth swallowed hard, then read on.

"No one knows for certain what happened. But when the new day dawned, an old man walking alone in the forest came across the deceased body of Claude Gautier, lying near the edge of the cliff above Devil's End.

"What struck the man most, he claims, was the look of utter terror on your father's face."

Garth lowered the letter, still gripping it tightly in his hand. For a long time he stared at the fire, the various phrases written by his great-grandmother replaying through his mind.

The look of terror on his face . . . There was a full moon. . . . The Power was present. . . .

And then one more phrase came into focus.

Your father died three nights ago. . . .

The implications of those words suddenly became clear. Quickly he checked the date written at the top of the letter.

Elizabeth Gautier had written it on December 24th.

That meant Garth's great-grandfather had died the night of the winter solstice, the same night on which there had been a full moon.

Panic rose up inside him. The winter solstice . . . a full moon . . . how often did those two events occur on the same night? He was certain it was a rarity. Yet it was happening once again, this year, in just four more nights.

The night of the final battle . . .

For the first time, Garth realized there was even more at stake than lifting the evil curse forever.

The winter solstice could well turn out to be the night he was destined to meet with his own demise.

CHAPTER
16

Fear gnawed at Miranda as she pulled open the door of the Overlook Town Hall. Tonight's committee meeting was guaranteed to be heated, with emotions running high.

Garth, she feared, could well end up at the center.

Yet she had to be there. She longed to protect him—even now, when his love for her, once a blazing fire, had been reduced to nothing more than ashes.

The last town meeting, called by Mayor Blackwell to allow local residents to air their views on the attacks, had been so well attended that the good-sized auditorium of the Overlook Opera House had been packed to the rafters. Miranda feared a similarly large turnout tonight. And so when she stepped into the entrance of the town hall and opened the door of the conference room, her stomach knotted with dread, she was relieved to see that tonight only two dozen or so had ventured out.

This room was much smaller, little more than a large office furnished with an oval-shaped table surrounded by chairs, the extra chairs pushed into every other available space. She took a seat in the corner, keeping her eyes down, hoping the proceedings would begin promptly. Within seconds, however, she realized she was not going to be so lucky. Dave Falco was already headed in her direction.

"I figured you'd be here tonight," he said with a sneer.

"Where's your friend?" Miranda glanced behind him, surprised Amy Patterson wasn't in tow.

"Where's *yours*?"

Anger rose inside her. But before she had a chance to respond, Officer Vale sat down next to her.

"Mind if I join you, Miranda?" she said, smiling.

"Not at all." She cast Dave a cold look. "Dave was just leaving."

"You'll be hearing from me later," he said, his eyes hard. "That, I can promise."

"Goodness, who's that?" asked Officer Vale.

"No one important." Miranda turned her attention to the police officer. "Are you one of the speakers?"

"No, I'm not here in any official capacity.

Tonight I've merely come as a concerned citizen.

"Besides," she went on, "from what I under-stand, the point of this meeting is simply for peo-ple to talk about how the town should approach the holiday celebration. I don't think there'll be much discussion of the attacks themselves."

Automatically Miranda's eyes traveled over to Dave. He was looking right at her as he whis-pered to Amy, who'd just come in. Corinne wasn't far behind.

"I hope not," she said softly.

Yet as she scanned the group, picking out Ms. Wallace, the clerk at the Overlook Public Library, and a few others she recognized, Miranda's heart suddenly grew even heavier. She'd just noticed two more familiar faces in the conference room: Margaret Donahue and Vir-ginia Swensen.

"The meeting will now come to order," said Mayor Blackwell, stepping up to the front of the room. "The reason I arranged this informal dis-cussion tonight is that some of you have expressed concerns to me about the appropriateness of carrying on with our usual town celebration this holiday season. Specifically, the events we're cons-idering are the annual winter carnival and the caroling on Christmas Eve. The reason for the controversy, of course, is the recent attacks on some of Overlook's young people—"

"Attacks!" Margaret Donahue called out

from her seat in front. "Try *murder!*"

"Mrs. Donahue, there will be sufficient time for everyone's comments to be addressed—"

"I have only one comment!" Mrs. Donahue cried, rising to her feet. "And that's that it's an insult to both the Swensens and the Davises for the town board even to *consider* proceeding with business as usual this Christmas!"

"Why not let the Swensens and the Davises speak for themselves?" someone else suggested calmly from the back of the room.

Miranda glanced up at the sound of the familiar voice. She was grateful to see Elinor standing in the doorway, still wearing her coat.

"Mr. and Mrs. Davis aren't here tonight," said Officer Vale. "But I understand they're in favor of the town proceeding with its usual holiday celebration."

"Oh, are they?" Mrs. Swensen stood up, her lips drawn into a straight line and her eyes bright. Immediately a hush fell over the crowd. "Maybe that's because their daughter is fine. She only suffered a few scars from her attack." With her hand she gestured vaguely toward Corinne. "Now my son, Andy, on the other hand—"

Officer Vale raised her hand. "Mrs. Swensen, believe me when I tell you that everyone in Overlook feels for you. We're all sorry for your loss. It was a terrible tragedy, one from which this town will never recover.

"But perhaps it's time to move on. It might even be a good thing for you and your husband to try to get past some of the grief—"

"What do you know about it?" Mrs. Swensen's face was red with rage. "How can I get past my grief until I can get my revenge?"

Miranda shrank back, horrified by the woman's fury. She was tempted to join Officer Vale in trying to placate her. But before she had a chance, Dave Falco stood up.

"We all want revenge!" he shouted, shaking his fist in the air. "Nobody in this town will be able to rest easy until the attacker is caught . . . and he gets his due!"

"Please," Mayor Blackwell interjected. "If we could get back to the matter at hand—"

"Why haven't the police caught the perpetrator?" Margaret Donahue demanded. Turning to Officer Vale, she added, "Why aren't you out there right now, scouring the woods, trying to find the killer?"

"I can assure you, Mrs. Donahue," the police officer replied in a controlled voice, "the police are doing everything in our power to trap the animal responsible for the attacks. We're confident that—"

Suddenly Amy stood up, her eyes blazing. "There's something I want to say. I have reason to believe that the attacker isn't an animal."

A murmur rose up from the room. Mayor

Blackwell held up both his hands in frustration. "I appreciate everyone's concerns. But if we can hold this discussion for another time, when—"

"And there's someone here who can identify him," Amy went on. "Somebody who not only saw him, but was one of his victims."

Miranda's heart was pounding so hard she was certain everyone in the room could hear it. She shut her eyes, knowing full well what was to come.

No, she thought. *Please . . . no.*

When she opened her eyes, she saw that Corinne was standing in front. Her face was white, her eyes wide and filled with anger.

"I saw him," she said, her voice low and rasping. "I remember now. It's all come back to me."

The room was silent. Everyone watched in fascination and horror as Corinne pulled up her sweater just enough to reveal the ugly red welts cutting through her flesh.

"I know who did this to me." Corinne's eyes traveled around the room, lighting upon Miranda as she exclaimed, "It was Garth Gautier! Miranda Campbell's boyfriend is responsible!"

"No!" Miranda gasped. "She's wrong! It wasn't Garth!"

"Your boyfriend!" Virginia Swensen had turned to face her, her hands clenched into tight fists. "I should have known you had something to do with this!"

"Order, please!" Mayor Blackwell demanded. "Everyone, sit down. This is not the proper forum for making accusations—"

"We want revenge!" Dave repeated. "We know there's something strange going on out there at Cedar Crest! He thought he could fool us, but we're on to him now!"

A sick feeling washed over Miranda. The room seemed to be growing smaller, the walls closing in on her. She could barely catch her breath. She longed to run, to get away from the panic that was rising inside her.

But she had to stay. She had no choice but to defend Garth . . . to try to convince these people to change their minds about seeking revenge against him.

"Most of you were at the last town meeting," she said, struggling to keep her voice from wavering. "You heard my father's testimony. He's a veterinarian, an expert on animals, and he said he was certain an animal was responsible for the attacks."

Pointing to Corinne, she added, "She's shown you her scars. You can see for yourself that they look like claw marks. How could a human being have been responsible for what was so clearly the result of an animal attack?"

"The answer," Amy shot back, "is that Garth Gautier is not just any 'human being.' I've done some research, and I've learned quite a bit about a mental illness called lycanthropy. A person who has this condition actually believes he turns into a wolf whenever there's a full moon."

Looking directly at Miranda, she said, "I believe that the mysterious intruder who came to this town right before the attacks began has this illness. Garth Gautier thinks he's a werewolf!"

"That's absurd," someone muttered.

"Is this documented?" a man who'd been silent up until that point asked. "Officer Vale, is this something the police have considered?"

"I have to agree with Miranda on this," Officer Vale replied. "The police department has great respect for Dr. Campbell's testimony. If he's convinced those markings were made by a large wolf, we have to weigh that evidence heavily."

"What about a person—somebody young, somebody big and strong—who brought an animal skin with him during his attacks?" Amy went on. "What if the attacker actually carried the pelt of a wolf into the forest, and used the paw of the wolf as his weapon?"

Her eyes narrowed. "Or what if he actually *dressed up* like a wolf, managing to convince his victims that he really *was* a wild animal?"

"Hey, I've seen a wolf around here," Dave Falco suddenly burst out. "Twice, in fact."

"Dave . . ." Miranda muttered.

But he acted as if he hadn't heard her. "Just last weekend I was driving around with a couple of my buddies and we swerved off the road when we saw a big wolf in the middle of the road. Nearly got ourselves killed, too. At least I thought it was a wolf at the time. But now that you mention it, it might've been a guy wearing a wolfskin. Yeah, I'm sure it could've been. Then there was this other time—"

"Dave." This time, Miranda spoke much more loudly. "I think everyone here has heard enough about this. Let's respect what Mayor Blackwell's been saying and move on to the discussion we're supposed to be having tonight."

"Wait. There's something else," a woman sitting on the side of the room said softly.

Miranda turned and paled as she saw Ms. Wallace raising her hand.

"I haven't said anything up until now, but I'm beginning to realize I may have kept silent too long."

"Yes, Ms. Wallace?" Mayor Blackwell said, his tone one of resignation. "What is it?"

"At first I thought I'd just been careless," Ms. Wallace mused. "Things at the library have been so confused lately. We're closing the museum, you know, making way for a computer center. . . . Anyway, I just assumed the wolfskin had been misplaced while we were packing up the Native American artifacts."

"Am I understanding this correctly?" Officer Vale asked. "You're saying that a wolfskin has been missing from the library?"

Mrs. Wallace nodded. "It's a beautiful piece. The complete pelt of a full-sized adult male, in perfect condition. The fur was so thick and soft, the most beautiful shade of silver-gray you've ever seen—"

"That's it!" Dave exclaimed. "That sounds exactly like the wolf I saw! I mean, the creature I thought at first was a wolf, but I now realize could have just as easily been some guy slinking around with an animal skin on his shoulders."

"I saw it too," Corinne insisted. "Gray fur. And light eyes. I don't remember the exact color. Brown, probably, or hazel."

The crowd was growing more and more agitated. Miranda looked around the room, desperate for a way of settling everyone down.

And then, another voice broke through the din.

"I saw a wolf as well," Elinor said, sounding calm and confident. "It started to attack me, then got scared and ran back into the woods. From the way it was behaving, I'd say it was the same wolf that attacked Andy and Corinne."

"Or else it was Garth, wearing the missing wolfskin," Dave insisted.

"It was probably Garth!" Amy cried. "It had to be!"

"No," Elinor returned. "It couldn't have been. The wolf that tried to attack me was unusual. It had golden fur. And its eyes were blue, the brightest, most distinctive eyes I've ever seen on an animal. I could see them perfectly because it was a clear night and the moon was particularly bright."

"Oh, yeah?" Dave countered. "You're just saying that to protect Garth. I've noticed that you and Miranda have become pretty chummy lately—"

"Excuse me, young man," Officer Vale interrupted, her voice tart. "I can verify that that's not the case at all. Elinor came into the police station a few days after she sighted the wolf. She described it in detail. According to the description she gave then, the wolf she saw did, indeed, have golden fur and blue eyes. To date, that's the only official statement that's been given to the police.

"Therefore, I'm afraid your lycanthropy theory isn't something the police can take very seriously," she finished, glancing first at Amy, then at Dave and Corinne. "It sounds as if there really is a wolf running around out there. One with its own fur—*golden* fur—and not some gray animal skin from the basement of the library."

Miranda noticed that Dave cast Elinor a hostile look. But he sat back down in his seat, apparently defeated.

She, meanwhile, felt a tremendous weight being lifted from her shoulders. As the mayor finally managed to turn the discussion to the Christmas Eve caroling, she had a difficult time concentrating on what the others were saying. She was too focused on Garth.

Officer Vale had come to his rescue—tonight. But while her testimony had done an excellent job of poking holes in Amy Patterson's incriminating theory, there was something else troubling her, something the police officer had done nothing to alleviate. And that was the anger of people like Dave and Amy and Virginia Swensen.

Their anger . . . and their desire for revenge.

"Thanks for coming to the meeting," Miranda said to Elinor as they walked out of town hall later that evening. The night was dark, the field of black overhead unlit by either stars or moonlight.

"I'm glad I did. Boy, Dave Falco's really got it out for Garth, hasn't he?" Elinor thought for a few seconds before adding, "I wonder why."

"It probably has something to do with Amy," Miranda said quickly. "The two of them are suddenly a hot item."

"So I gathered. And I guess she's still trying to get back at you—for no other reason than you happen to be Bobby's ex-girlfriend." Elinor sighed. "Why can't people like that just leave well enough alone? She's trouble. So's Dave.

Together . . . well, who knows what they're capable of? Just be careful you don't get in their way, Miranda."

"I'll try."

When they reached the point where they had to go off in different directions to get home, Elinor offered, "Do you want me to walk home with you? You could drive me back to my house." She glanced up at the black, starless sky. "I don't know if I'm just imagining things, but it seems unusually dark tonight."

"It's cloudy, that's all." More to herself than to Elinor, Miranda added, "There's going to be a full moon in five more nights."

Elinor laughed hollowly. "You're beginning to sound like Amy. Next thing you know, *you'll* start believing Garth is a werewolf!"

All of a sudden a sob escaped the back of Miranda's throat.

"What's the matter?" Elinor demanded. "Are you all right?"

"Oh, Elinor," Miranda cried, "Garth and I broke up. It's over!"

"Oh, no! What happened?"

"I'm not sure. All I know is that he's certain he's no longer in love with me."

"Do you still love him, Miranda?"

She nodded, brushing at the tears running down her face. "Yes. I love Garth in a way I never knew it was possible to love someone.

He's everything I want. I—I can't imagine life without him."

"Then tell him," Elinor said gently. "Let him know what's in your heart."

"He already knows. But it's too late."

Miranda hesitated, thinking for a long time before she continued. She desperately wanted to tell someone her secret, the secret she'd been harboring for so long. All of a sudden, it seemed like too great a burden to bear alone.

Haltingly, she began to speak. "Elinor, there's something I want to tell you. A terrible secret— so terrible that you're the only person in the entire world I trust with it."

"You know I won't tell anyone."

"It's more than that. I—I also want to be certain you won't pass judgment. That you'll just accept what I have to say without casting blame or . . . or rejecting the whole idea."

"I'll try, Miranda."

Miranda took a deep breath, and when she looked up she saw that Elinor was looking at her expectantly.

"You know those accusations about lycanthropy that Amy's been making? The way she's been going around telling everyone that Garth believes he's a werewolf?"

Elinor nodded.

Miranda's heart was pounding. She knew she was taking an enormous risk . . . yet at the same time she trusted Elinor, completely and without reservation. Her eyes cast downward, she went on.

"Well, Garth doesn't *believe* he's a werewolf. He's the victim of a curse that's haunted his family for hundreds of years. Elinor, Garth *is* a werewolf. Every time there's a full moon, he comes under the power of an evil force, shapeshifting into a huge wolf. It's out of his control, a horrible legacy he's had to bear ever since he was fifteen years old."

She paused to catch her breath. Her heart was pounding so hard she felt as if she'd been running as fast as she could. "Garth was the one responsible for those attacks, Elinor. He killed Andy Swensen and he mauled Corinne. He killed that bear the police found in the woods. And he was the wolf you and I saw the night of the play's opening, the wolf that nearly attacked you.

"But it wasn't really Garth! That's what you have to understand! It's—it's something he can't control. The dark legacy of the Gautier family is what's really responsible. And he and I are desperate to lift the curse, to undo it once and for all. We've come to believe it's our destiny, but now I'm not so sure. Without Garth's love I just don't know if I can fight anymore."

And then Miranda was silent. She was exhausted, as if finally letting go of what she'd been holding in for so long had required every ounce of strength she possessed. She did feel relieved, just as she'd anticipated. But she also felt fearful. Anxiously she glanced over at Elinor.

"Do you believe me?" Miranda asked.

"Yes. I believe you." Suddenly Elinor threw her arms around Miranda. "Oh, Miranda! What a terrible thing you've been living with! How you must have suffered! But now I understand."

"Can you accept Garth for what he is?"

"If you love him, Miranda, I can accept him."

"Oh, Elinor. I'm so glad. Thank you!"

"Miranda," she said earnestly, gripping her by both shoulders, "what you've told me makes me realize you can't give up. You've got to hang in there and fight. You have to fight to release Garth from the family curse, but also to save your love.

"It's special. It's magical. If the two of you really were thrown together by fate, destined to end a curse that's lasted hundreds of years, you have to overcome whatever obstacles are standing in your way."

"But Garth's love for me has faded!"

"Give it time, Miranda. Don't give up. You still have a battle ahead of you, one that's going to take all your concentration and all your energy. See it through to the end, and never for a moment lose hope. When you and Garth come out of it, your love may triumph."

"I hope you're right." Hugging Elinor,

Miranda felt a glimmer of hope for the first time since that terrible day at Cedar Crest.

Elinor put a comforting arm around Miranda. "Come on. I'll walk you home. You shouldn't be alone right now."

"Thanks, but I'm fine. Really." Through her tears, Miranda forced a smile. "I think I just want to go home and climb into bed."

"Well . . . if you're sure . . ."

"I'm sure." Miranda turned away, then hesitated. "Elinor?" she called into the darkness.

"Yes, Miranda?"

"Thank you for being such a good friend."

"I haven't done anything," Elinor replied somberly. "I just want you to live out your destiny."

It wasn't until Miranda was walking down one of the quiet residential streets of Overlook that she realized it really was an unusually dark night.

There's probably a storm brewing, she mused, glancing up at the pitch-black canopy of the evening sky.

She quickened her pace, suddenly in a hurry to get home.

And then she stopped, her ears pricked.

"Who's there?" she demanded, turning to see if she really had heard a footstep. She tried to sound forceful, but her words came out shaky and weak.

The response was a scraping sound, followed by a small burst of light. Instantly the pungent smell of sulfur stung her nostrils.

"What do you want?" she cried.

"It's kind of dark out tonight," Dave Falco's mocking voice returned. "Thought I'd do you a favor and help light your way." Holding the flame slightly under his chin so that his face was illuminated but cast in strange shadows, he added, "I know how much you like fire, Miranda."

In a sudden jerking motion, he tossed the lit match at her. The flame was out by the time it left his hand, but she stepped away automatically, letting out a little cry.

Dave laughed. "What's the matter?" he cackled. "Afraid of getting burned? *You*, Miranda?"

He tossed another lighted match at her, this one remaining lit and landing near her feet. Once again she jumped backward.

"Stop it!" she insisted, her voice edged with fear. "Get out of here, Dave."

"'Get out of here, Dave,'" he repeated in a singsong voice. "Why, Miranda, you haven't asked me lately how Mark's doing. Don't tell me you're not interested."

"Of course I'm interested. How is he?"

"Mark is—naw, I'm not going to tell you. Because I don't believe you really care."

He lit another match, holding this one up to her face. She tried to run, but he grabbed hold of her arm. "Hey, where do you think you're going?"

"Dave, let go of me. You're hurting me."

"Mark knows all about getting hurt. You do care about how he's doing, Miranda, don't you?"

She nodded, swallowing hard. The flame was only inches away from her face.

"I can't hear you," Dave taunted. His dark eyes glinted in the light from the fire, and his lips were drawn into a sneer.

"I—I care. How is Mark?"

"Ouch!" The flame had burned down too close to his fingers. Dave dropped the match. He dropped her arm to light another, and she began to run.

He was too fast for her. Within seconds he'd caught up, gripping her arm so tightly she uttered a cry of pain.

"Don't be in such a hurry. You and I have still got a lot to talk about."

"My mother is expecting me," Miranda insisted. "If I'm not home in about thirty seconds, she's going to come looking for me."

He didn't seem to have heard. "Listen, Miranda," he hissed, his face right up against hers, "I don't know what kind of black magic you've got up your sleeve. But I want you to know I'm not afraid of you—or that wolfman character, either."

"Look, just let me go."

"When I'm good and ready."

"Dave, please," she begged. "Let go of me."

And then a deep voice cut through the night. "Leave her alone."

Miranda started at the familiar sound. She was struck by the presence of something unfamiliar in it, an angry edge she hadn't heard before. Glancing up, even against the dark backdrop of night she could see a furious glint in Garth's eyes.

"I said, leave her alone."

"Well, well, well," Dave said. "Garth to the rescue." His tone was jeering, but Miranda detected a note of fear underlying it.

The two boys stood face to face, their eyes locked together in a malevolent gaze for what seemed to Miranda an eternity. And then, relief rushing over her so quickly that her knees felt weak, she felt Dave's grip on her arm loosen.

"Why don't you take your matches and get out of here." Garth spat out his words.

Dave just glared at him. Miranda held her breath. Then, finally, he took a step backward.

"Okay, I'll leave," he growled. "For *now*. But don't start thinking this is over," he went on, his dark eyes still fixed on Garth's. "Believe me, Gautier, you've still got a ways to go before you've seen the last of me."

CHAPTER
17

Miranda lay stretched across her bed late Saturday afternoon, staring at the blank pages of her journal. She was overcome by such a sense of anticipation, the unsettling feeling of uncertainty and fear that accompanied the endless waiting, that she'd tried to seek comfort in pouring her thoughts out on paper.

Yet no words would come. Her heart fluttered anxiously, her thoughts were scattered. Concentrating was impossible.

She abandoned her diary, standing up and pacing around the room. The winter solstice was only three days away. She could think of nothing else. She wanted the time to pass quickly, so she could end the agonizing wait; at the same time, she dreaded the arrival of the night of the final battle, wishing it would never come.

When her mother appeared in the doorway of her bedroom, she started.

"I'm sorry," Mrs. Campbell said with a smile. "I didn't mean to interrupt you."

"I wasn't busy. Besides, I could use some company."

Her mother sat down on the edge of the bed. "You looked as if you were a million miles away."

"I guess I was." Miranda tried to keep her tone light. "But I'm back now."

"Good. I was wondering if by any chance you were free tonight."

"I don't have any plans. I thought I'd stay in and catch up on some homework."

"How about going out to dinner with your father and me?"

"That sounds like fun." The distraction would be welcome, she realized. Her curiosity was also piqued by the invitation to go out as a family. This would be the first time they had done that in weeks. "Anything special?"

"Not really. We just thought we'd start finalizing our plans for the holidays. I looked at the calendar this morning and realized that Christmas is only a few days away." Mrs. Campbell smiled.

When Miranda's father picked them up and suggested that she be the one to choose the restaurant, she didn't hesitate.

"This is so lovely!" Mrs. Campbell exclaimed

as the three of them were seated at a quiet corner table at the romantic country inn Miranda had come to with Jeff Jordan. "I don't remember the last time I ate here."

"I do." Miranda's tone was casual. "It was a little over a year ago. You and Daddy came here to celebrate your wedding anniversary."

She noticed her mother casting a knowing glance at her father.

"Yes, I remember," Miranda's father said, his eyes glowing with a strange intensity.

Mrs. Campbell blushed.

After they'd ordered, Miranda asked, "So what are we going to do on Christmas this year?"

"I'd love an old-fashioned holiday," said Mrs. Campbell. "Plenty of candles, a fire roaring in the fireplace, quiet evenings singing carols and stringing cranberries and popcorn to decorate the house . . ."

Miranda sighed. "It sounds perfect."

"Honey, maybe you'd like Garth to join us. If he's not spending the day with his family, that is."

Miranda pretended to be absorbed in rearranging the linen napkin in her lap. "Thanks, Mom, but I don't think that will work out."

She glanced up at her mother, afraid of what her reaction would be. But she simply nodded.

"I have yet to do anything about shopping for presents," Mrs. Campbell went on. "I thought we'd go up to Portland. . . ."

" 'We?' "

"Your mother and I haven't been up there for quite some time," Dr. Campbell said casually. "Doing a little Christmas shopping sounds like the ideal excuse."

Miranda hesitated, wondering if she dared say what was on her mind. Her parents seemed to be getting along so well, and she knew that as time went on they'd been spending more and more time together. . . .

"Mom, Dad," she began, choosing her words carefully, "maybe you'd rather I kept out of this, but . . ." She took a deep breath. "Am I imagining things, or have the two of you reached a sort of truce?"

"I hope it's more than a truce," Dr. Campbell replied earnestly. "Miranda, your mother and I have been seeing a marriage counselor over the past few weeks. We've been trying to learn how to talk to each other."

"How to listen to each other too," her mother interjected.

"We're both committed to finding a way to work out our problems. We've been learning a lot about each other lately. About ourselves, as well."

"Do you know what I'd really like for a Christmas present?" Miranda suddenly burst out. "I'd like Dad to move back home."

She expected her parents to protest. Instead, her father took her mother's hand.

"We'll see," he said, smiling mysteriously.

Even though she was exhausted, it took Miranda a long time to fall asleep Saturday night. Her dinner with her parents had left her feeling optimistic about her family's future for the first time in months. She lay in bed, imagining how it would feel to have the three of them back together again, relieved to have something reassuring to think about. How good it felt, knowing that at least one part of her life was beginning to work out.

If only the other aspects could be resolved as well, she thought. Lying in the dark, she discovered that her escape from her ruminations about Garth and what still lay ahead had been short-lived. Her heart still ached with love for him, a love that went unreturned. Yet her commitment to try to release him from the curse that tormented him remained strong. Not even the terrible fear she felt in her heart deterred her.

She finally drifted off, expecting her dreams to be comforting. Instead, she felt she was being pulled down into a whirlpool, sinking deeper and deeper into an abyss that seemed to have no end. She had the sensation of falling, falling. . . .

Suddenly Miranda's eyes flew open. Her heart was racing, adrenaline pumping through her veins so rapidly she could barely catch her breath. An air of expectation hung in the room, so heavy it was almost palpable.

She lay in bed, her senses alert, yet not quite sure if she were dreaming. Her hair streamed across her pillow, and the blankets were a disheveled mass at the foot of the bed. She stayed very still, her mind not yet able to focus as she struggled out of the disoriented state of being half asleep, half awake.

Sitting up in bed, she glanced around the room. Pitch-blackness surrounded her, the darkness of the night outside the window broken by neither moonlight nor starlight. It was midnight, she saw, checking the glowing numbers of the clock next to her bed. She'd been asleep only a little more than an hour. Yet her fatigue had vanished.

And then she felt their presence.

"Who's there?" she cried.

She was not surprised when no answer came.

Fear gripped her as she sat alone in the darkness. The sound of rhythmic breathing, so gentle it was barely audible, filled the room. Desperately she tried to discern who—or what— was there with her.

And then Miranda felt a rush of warmth. It enveloped her like a cloak, making her feel protected.

Then she understood. They had come for her. It was time for the good narnauks to prepare her for the final battle.

Come, Miranda. Come with us.

The voices were softer than whispers. She heard them not with her ears, but with her mind.

Slowly she rose from her bed. From the open window came a sharp gust of wind, causing her white flannel nightgown to billow. She was aware that its iciness should have assaulted her, but it did not. Instead, that same warmth shielded her.

She moved barefoot across the floor, surprised that she could not feel the hardness of the wood beneath her feet.

She realized then she was suspended somewhere between the world of dreams and the world of reality.

Come with us, Miranda.

Feeling as if she were floating, she went down the stairs and through the silent house. She placed her hand on the knob of the front door, yet could not feel it.

As she stepped through the front door, she observed her own actions with detachment, surprised but not at all afraid. Miranda understood that all along she'd been expecting them to come for her, that she'd been waiting, knowing deep inside that in order to prepare herself for the final battle, she would have to succumb totally to their will.

Outside, the wind was strong. The folds of her nightgown whipped around her legs. Her bare feet traveled confidently over stones and grass, gravel and blacktop, her flesh feeling none of the sensations borne of this earth. With determination she walked, knowing precisely where she was headed, her steps unwavering as she headed toward the forest.

All around her played the music of the night. The cry of the nocturnal animals, hunting down their prey. The whistling wind, weaving through the trees. The crashing of the waves of the sea, violent and untamed. The rustling cedars, swaying back and forth.

Gradually she became aware of another sound: the pounding of drums, far in the distance. The rhythmic beat was enticing, pulling her closer and closer. Moving with that same determination, putting one foot in front of the other with the dreamy motions of a sleepwalker, Miranda made her way through the woods.

The pounding grew louder. Still she kept on, irresistibly drawn to the incessant pulsing. When she passed through a thick clump of trees and entered a clearing, she was not surprised to see a low white building in its center. The white surface of the outer walls was painted with bright colors, red and green and blue, the bold designs of animals emphasized with strokes of black. All around, torches burned, casting the building in oblique light and oddly shaped shadows.

The Big House. Exactly as Featherwoman had prophesied.

At one end was a totem pole. Miranda recognized it immediately as the totem pole from the center of town.

Tonight the faces of the animals carved into the log were alive, their bright eyes glinting in the light from the fire, their mouths drawn back into angry snarls.

The eyes of the wolf bored into hers.

Tonight she did not look away. She met the wolf's gaze head-on, feeling no fear.

The drums were louder now, the pounding so forceful that the earth vibrated. They called to her, the steady throbbing beckoned to her.

Miranda knew the drums were beating for her.

Slowly she walked toward the door. She paused, for a moment contemplating the momentousness of what she was about to do.

And then she entered.

Darkness enveloped her, made forbidding by the loud drumming, so close now that its steady beating seemed to invade her very soul. She was part of it, caught up in a rhythm so powerful it banished every thought from her mind.

Slowly her eyes adjusted to the dim light inside the Big House. Torches illuminated the long, low building, the same eerie shadows and patches of flickering light she'd seen outside the building dancing across the whitewashed walls.

The brightly colored images of animals covered their surface. Blinking hard and then studying the crude pictures, Miranda saw that they were all wolves.

Just like the images on the totem, they appeared to be alive, their hungry eyes fixed upon her.

Gradually the moving shadows came into focus. Men and women dressed in animal skins, their sinewy arms and legs and torsos painted with the same bold shades of red and green and black, danced to the beat of the drums, their movements impassioned. Many of them wore masks, animal heads with their mouths contorted into the same cruel grimaces as those on the totem. Feathers and twigs and pieces of bark edged the giant faces, streaming through the air as the dancers twisted their bodies in time to the pounding.

Miranda could feel her own body responding. The urge to dance, to move her body in the same manner as the others, was too strong to resist. Tentatively at first, quickly growing more and more confident, she copied the rhythmic motions of those around her.

Miranda could feel her strength increasing. Rather than growing tired as she joined the others, moving into the circle they'd formed, she discovered she was energized by the movements.

Around and around the circle she went, feeling a surge of power rising up from deep inside her. Her head cleared, all thoughts of her worldly life disappearing. Instead a sense of serenity took her over, lifting her spirits so that she was bathed by a kind of joy unlike anything she had ever before experienced.

Suddenly she became aware of a change in the air. Jerking her head around, she glanced into the center of the circle formed by the dancers.

A wolf stood in the middle, merely a few feet away, crouching and staring at her.

Miranda saw immediately that the others did not seem to notice. Only she saw the wolf.

Her initial alarm quickly melted away. In its place was understanding.

This was her totem.

The supernatural animal being was appearing before her to give her its special powers.

The spirit of the wolf had appeared to instill in her the strength and the ability she would need to fight the final battle.

Along with that flash of understanding came a new feeling. The sensation of being lifted, of rising up off the ground, took her over. She felt a lightness, a weightlessness, that enabled her to see her body in a whole new way. . . .

The power is mine.

Her mind was clear, capable of thoughts un- like those she'd ever had before. She finally possessed the understanding she had craved for so long. . . .

The power is mine.

Her soul felt cleansed, her spirit brand-new. . . .

The power is mine.

Miranda threw back her head and closed her eyes, luxuriating in the sensation of strength, of purity, of understanding.

At last, she was prepared for the final battle.

Silence surrounded her. The realization that the drums had ceased startled her. Miranda jerked her head forward, letting out a little cry as she opened her eyes.

She was still in the forest, but the Big House was gone. The fire, the dancers, the animal images . . . vanished.

She glanced down and saw she was still dressed only in her nightgown. Her bare feet were cradled by a clump of soft, cool grass. The wind was gentle now, ruffling through her white nightgown, flowing through her hair. It was welcome, its presence like that of a friend.

Miranda became aware of a new sound: the gurgling of a brook. She glanced to the side and saw she was standing at the place in which she and Garth had once had a picnic. It seemed so long ago. . . .

The moon had emerged, peeking out from behind the clouds, illuminating the clearing just enough for her to see the dark green grass, the rich brown riverbank, the silvery waters of the stream. It was so beautiful, so peaceful. . . .

Suddenly something caught her eye. A flash of light glinted off the rushing waters.

Curious, she edged closer to the edge of the brook. Something at the bottom was reflecting the pale moonlight.

At first, Miranda assumed it was simply an unusual stone. Or perhaps some form of plant life, picking up the light in an unusual way. Yet she was drawn to it, so much so she could not turn away.

She leaned forward, trying to get a better look. The shiny object was half hidden, most of it plunged deep into the soft sediment lining the bottom of the river. The article was long and slender. Her curiosity piqued even further, she leaned forward and tried to grab hold of it.

The object was just beyond her reach. The more she stretched her arm toward it, the further away it seemed. She had the impression it was moving away from her.

It must be the current, she thought. The odd manner in which the object, whatever it is, keeps moving away, just out of reach . . .

She knew she should simply let it go. Yet something inside would not allow her to. Miranda could not resist the urge to know what it was. She had to free the object. She longed to hold it in her hands . . . to possess it.

Without hesitation, she pulled up her night-gown a few inches and stepped into the stream. She expected it to be icy; instead, it was enticingly warm. It swallowed her feet up to the ankles, the rushing waters lapping up along the hem of her nightgown. Nothing deterred her. Instead, she took a few steps toward the place where she'd spotted the object.

And then panic gripped her. It was gone.

Desperately she thrust her hands into the silky sediment, her fingers plunging down deeply as in vain they sought the coveted object. Fine grains of sand passed through her fingers, along with hard chunks of rock. But the long, silver object was nowhere to be found. It had been lost to the swirling waters of the mountain stream, the soft ooze at the bottom that so eagerly swallowed up anything deposited there.

Miranda let out a cry. In a sudden flash of understanding, she knew what the shiny object had been.

The knife.

It had been returned to her. The good narnauks had put it in her path—or at least they had tried.

Yet their plan had been foiled.

Miranda's heart was heavy as she turned away. Stepping up onto the bank, she dried her feet on the tall grass. Whereas lightness had once lifted her upward, confusion now dragged her down.

She had been infused with the power . . . yet even that power had not been enough. The third item necessary to triumph in the end was still lost to her.

Trudging home through the woods, Miranda was assaulted by the cold. No longer did she possess a shield against the icy wind whipping through the forest. Her bare feet were cut and scraped by the rough stones and sharp twigs over which they trod.

Never before had she felt so alone.

"Why have you abandoned me?" she cried aloud, her words instantly swallowed up by the wind.

But in her heart, she did not give up. She had seen too much. She still carried within her the power of the wolf. The transformation that had taken place inside the Big House had left its mark. Of this she was now certain.

When she reached her house, Miranda was overcome with fatigue. It took all her strength to lift her heavy legs up the stairs, toward her bedroom. The same stillness lay over the house. Nothing had been disturbed. Nothing had changed.

Yet she still had the sense that *she* had changed, in a way so dramatic she could never quite go back to the way she'd been before. . . .

She entered her bedroom. And then she saw it.

The pale moonlight streamed through the window, illuminating only the bed. The white sheets glowed with an eerie luminescence.

Lying on the bed, tucked into the pillow in the same spot in which not long before her head had been nestled, was the knife.

Letting out a little cry, Miranda rushed over to the bed. Reverently she picked it up, holding it in both hands, examining it.

How it gleamed! While once the silver blade had been tarnished, the wooden handle dull, it looked brand-new. The blade, now razor sharp, glinted in the wan moonlight, the surface bright and even, the few imperfections that had once marred the metal surface now smoothed over.

The handle was highly polished, the wood rich and freshly oiled.

And then she noticed the change.

When she'd first found the knife, the picture carved into the handle had been of two wolves, confronting each other face-to-face.

The picture was still the same. The heads of both wolves were molded into the wood. But the emphasis was completely different. The evil wolf, its head dark and its mouth pulled back into a menacing sneer, had nearly faded into the background, little more than a shadow.

The other wolf, meanwhile, had taken on much greater clarity. Now, unlike before, it was the dominant figure in the wood carving.

Miranda clasped the handle tightly in her hand, clamping her eyes shut and raising her head upward toward the heavens.

"Thank you," she cried.

As she spoke those two words, that same surge of power she'd felt at the Big House rushed over her. She felt strengthened, as if merely grasping the knife was once again infusing her with that special energy.

And then, through her closed eyelids, shined a brilliant light.

Slowly Miranda opened her eyes. The light was all around, warm and bright, enveloping her in a protective bubble. It illuminated the room. Outside, through the window, she could see that it lit up the bark of the trees, glinted off the needles of the cedars. The world was suddenly radiant, glowing with a light so brilliant she understood its source was in some other world.

Never before had Miranda felt so alive, so much at peace.

She glanced down at the knife, still held firmly in both hands. It was luminescent, emitting the same warmth, the same energy, as the light that bathed the room.

And then she understood. It was true she possessed the power she needed to fight the final battle. Yet that was not enough. She still needed the good narnauks in order to triumph. And they were there to help her, to lead the way.

The bad narnauks, their enemies, had not given up. Still they sought to thwart them at every turn. But the good spirits were not going to succumb. They were determined to fight, to see this mission through. Never would they leave Miranda's side.

This, they had told her through their actions.

She knew no sleep would come to her tonight. Yet she climbed back into bed, the knife tucked underneath her pillow.

As she did, she glanced at the clock. The red numbers glowed the time: twelve, zero, one.

Her heart raced. Only one minute had passed. Frantic, she reached down and felt the bottoms of her feet.

The skin was perfectly smooth, unmarred by scratches or cuts.

Next she checked the hem of her nightgown.

It was completely dry.

What if it never happened? What if it was all just a dream . . . ?

Panic rising from deep inside, Miranda ran her fingers underneath the pillow.

She clutched the wooden handle of the knife tightly in her hand. "Thank you," she murmured.

CHAPTER
18

Miranda sat cross-legged on the floor of her bedroom Sunday evening, staring at the diary lying open in front of her. Tonight, no words would come. Her agitation was too great for her to concentrate on writing.

The winter solstice was only two days away.

Her eyes traveled to the window. The moon was large, almost a perfect circle, its brightness seeming to mock her as it peered into her room. The wind howled fiercely, shrieking and whooshing like a band of ghosts. When darkness fell late that afternoon, a bitter cold had burst into the air, an unusual iciness rising off the pounding waves of the Pacific.

Something else hovered in the air, as well . . . something she couldn't identify, but which was nonetheless unmistakable. Whatever it was, it cast an ominous feeling over the night, as if some danger, some nameless threat, were lurking out there, waiting to pounce.

When the silence was shattered by the ringing of the telephone, Miranda jumped. She laughed nervously at her reaction, trying to banish some of her anxiety. Yet her heart still beat quickly as she picked up the receiver.

"Good evening, Miss Miranda," Jeff Jordan greeted her flirtatiously.

"Jeff!" His phone call caught her completely off guard.

"I hope you're not busy."

"No, I—"

"You sound distracted."

"Actually, I was daydreaming."

"About me, I hope."

Dismayed, Miranda said, "Oh, Jeff . . . I think you and I need to have a talk."

She immediately sensed him growing tense. "I can tell I'd better brace myself for bad news."

"Jeff, I can't go out with you again."

There was a long silence on the other end of the line. "But I thought we got along well together. I thought we had fun." He paused before adding, "I know I did."

"Yes," she said hoarsely. "I did too."

"Why am I getting the feeling all this has something to do with the other guy you'd been seeing?"

When Miranda remained silent, he added, "Is he back on the scene?"

"No." She shut her eyes tightly to hold back the tears. "It's not that."

How could she ever explain that even though she'd been left with a gaping hole in her heart, there was still no room for love—not for Jeff, not for anyone? Her feelings for Garth were still too strong. Then there was that glimmer of hope, however tiny, planted by Elinor's advice about not giving up. . . .

"Jeff, you have to understand that it's not you. I like you, and I hope we can still be friends."

"Friends," Jeff repeated with a little laugh. "Well, if that's the best I can do, I guess I'll just have to get used to it."

"We'll be working together at the Limelight, don't forget. We've still got a lot of rehearsals ahead of us."

"Somehow, I'd been hoping for more. You're very special, Miranda. And after the run of the play is long past, even after we've gone our separate ways, I'll never forget you."

After Miranda hung up the phone, a feeling of loneliness came over her. She went downstairs in search of her mother, but discovered a note saying she'd gone out.

She was about to head back upstairs, determined to confront the blank pages of her journal once again, when she heard someone pounding on the front door. Frowning, she peered through the living-room window, then rushed to the door to open it.

"Miranda!" Elinor cried breathlessly. "I tried calling you, but your line was busy. So I came running over—"

"I'm sorry. I was on the phone." She noticed then the distraught look on Elinor's face. "What's wrong?"

"You've got to come, Miranda." She grabbed her by the arm. "It's Garth."

Miranda froze. "Has something happened to him?"

"Not yet. But there's an angry mob heading toward Cedar Crest, led by Dave Falco."

Miranda had already grabbed her jacket and was heading out the door.

"Should we drive or take our bikes?"

"We'll go through the woods," Miranda said. "I know a shortcut."

Hurrying through the forest, her heart pounded and her breaths came in gasps. Her mind raced so fast she felt as if she were in a dream—or more accurately, a terrible nightmare.

"How many people are there?" she demanded in a voice edged with hysteria.

"I'm not sure," Elinor returned. "All I know is that when I went into the Overlook Grocery about a half-hour ago to pick up something for my mother, I overheard Margaret Donahue talking about it to Mr. Henry. She was on her way over there herself."

Miranda didn't respond. Her thoughts were racing too fast for her to formulate a coherent response.

Garth! she kept thinking, over and over again. *Oh, please, let him be all right. Don't let them hurt him!*

When she reached the end of Winding Way, rushing onto the property of Cedar Crest with Elinor in tow, her heart stopped. A crowd of people stood in the driveway—fifty or sixty, at least. They surrounded the front door, many with their arms raised in the air as they shook their fists angrily.

Several of them carried torches, the flickering orange-red light from the flames illuminating their faces, casting their features in an eerie, unnatural glow. Even from a few hundred feet away, Miranda could see the fury in their expressions.

She could hear their enraged cries, as well.

"Show your face, you coward!"

"Come on out . . . or we'll come in to get you!"

"It's time to pay for what you've done!"

Watching the angry mob, Miranda became aware that Elinor was gripping her arm. "We'd better go back and call the police," Elinor said.

"No. There isn't time."

"Miranda," Elinor pleaded. "You can't stay here. It isn't safe for you!"

"You go. Call the police. I'm going in."

"Miranda, you can't—"

"I have to. He needs me."

And then she broke free of Elinor's grasp, heading toward the crowd.

"Miranda!" Elinor cried. But her words were immediately swallowed up by the wind.

Miranda moved toward the crowd, taking care to stay behind, where she was less likely to be noticed. Shielded by the mass of bodies, she watched. She saw Amy and Corinne and Margaret Donahue. Her heartbeat quickened even more when she saw Dave Falco standing up front, right outside the front door of Cedar Crest. In his hand was a burning plank of wood.

"Let's torch this place!" he shouted, brandishing the weapon he carried tightly in his fist.

"Yeah!" cried his friend Alan, breaking out from the crowd. "C'mon, Carl. Let's do it!"

"Somebody stop them!" Miranda cried.

No one stepped forward from the crowd, or even said a word. Horrified, she watched as Dave began walking toward Cedar Crest, firmly gripping his torch, his mouth twisted into an angry grimace.

"No!" Miranda cried. This time, her voice was barely audible. She knew it was no use. She was powerless against their anger, and no one was willing to come to her aid.

At least she thought there was no one.

Suddenly she gasped. Miranda watched wide-eyed as a single person stepped out of the crowd, his head held high, his expression determined.

"I think this has gone far enough," Bobby said, placing himself between Dave and the house. His voice was firm, yet not at all antagonistic. "Come on, Dave. Why don't you call off the witch hunt and go on home?"

He walked toward Dave, reaching for the torch. For a moment, a look of surprise crossed Dave's face. And then, as Bobby grew near, he stretched out his arm. In a sudden, jerking movement, he struck Bobby across the side of the head.

Miranda screamed as he fell to the ground. Pushing her way through the crowd, she went to his side. She fell to her knees, gently placing her hands on Bobby's face.

"Well, look who's here," Dave jeered. "The Bride of Frankenstein. Or maybe I should say the Bride of the Wolfman."

"Get out of here!" Miranda rose, standing so close to Dave their eyes were mere inches away. "Get out before it's too late!"

He let out a cold laugh. "It's already too late!" Still grasping the torch in one hand, Dave made a wide sweeping gesture with the other. "The police don't seem to care that there's a psychopath living in our town. So we have no choice but to take matters into our own hands."

"But someone's going to get hurt!"

"*Now* you've got the idea."

Suddenly Dave thrust out his arm, touching his torch to one of the shutters framing the window. Immediately the dry wood caught fire. With horrible efficiency the wind picked it up and carried it to the other shutter. Panic rising inside, Miranda rushed over to him, pulling on his arm.

"Stop, Dave! Stop! You've gone crazy!"

He didn't seem to have heard her. Instead, he called over his shoulder, "Come on, Alan. Get over here, Carl. Let's get this over with!"

His two friends joined him in igniting the building, all three of them hopping from place to place, touching their torches to the crumbling edifice that had once been magnificent. Within seconds flames leaped around Cedar Crest, their white-hot tongues encircling the house. They climbed up the bushes and the trees, stretching higher and higher, gaining strength with everything they devoured. They lapped at the wooden shutters, eating away at the slats, causing the windows to shatter and the draperies to ignite with ferocity. The front door caught fire, succumbing quickly and leaving a gaping black hole behind. The gray stones of Cedar Crest were scorched, thick black smoke destroying their surface with long destructive fingers while inside, the fire began to tear through the house.

It was a sickening sight. As she watched, something inside Miranda crumpled.

"No!" she cried, falling to her knees. She held out her hands imploringly. Tears streamed down her cheeks, and her stomach lurched. Yet she was unable to look away from the horrifying inferno before her.

"The fire trucks will never make it up here," she heard someone behind her declare in a satisfied voice.

"No way," someone else agreed. "Can you see them making those curves on Winding Way?"

And then she heard someone behind her, standing in the crowd, cry out, "Now he'll have to leave Overlook!"

"Leave?" a new voice returned. "He's not going anywhere!"

Miranda snapped her head around. She recognized that voice; it belonged to Andy Swensen's mother. In the eerie, flickering light of the flames, she could see the smug expression on her face.

"What are you talking about?" the first voice demanded.

Virginia Swensen's eyes glowed. "He's *in* there! Up in the *tower*!"

Miranda wasn't aware of making the decision to go in after him. All she knew was that she was suddenly running, the sick feeling overtaking her, her mind racing faster than ever as she embarked on the mission she knew without reservation she had to pursue.

"Stop her!" she heard someone scream.

"She's gone berserk!" another voice from the crowd yelled out.

"Miranda! You'll get killed in there!"

She heard what they were saying, but their words did nothing to deter her. Instead she ran toward Cedar Crest. At first she was gripped by a terrible panic. But then, as she neared the mansion, her skin burning from the heat of the flames, her eyes stinging from the acrid smoke, her fear began slipping away.

In its place was a feeling of calm. A feeling of certainty that this was the right thing to do.

Yes, Miranda. Go to him.

The words brushed by her ear like a soft spring wind, so gentle they were almost like a caress. Her limbs felt light, yet at the same time so strong she knew she was powerful enough to perform even the most demanding feat. Her eyes were wide open, no longer bothered by the smoke. And the heat from the fire was suddenly comforting, beckoning toward her, welcoming her into its bosom.

"Garth," she said. That simple word, that single syllable, infused her with such power that the rest of the world slipped away.

She was aware that they were still behind her,

watching—some with fear, others with curiosity. She could hear the beating of their hearts, feel the pulse of the blood rushing through their veins.

She could feel some of them willing her to turn away, to come back to them.

Miranda took another step, then another, toward the house. Already the real world behind her was slipping away, farther and farther with each step she took.

Yes, Miranda. Yes.

She had reached the front door, the blackened hole framed by fire. Cedar Crest invited her in, its charred surface beckoning to her, its intense warmth too inviting to resist.

She stopped. *Danger!* a voice inside her cried. *Go back, Miranda. Go back.*

Yet that voice was suddenly drowned out by music, the most beautiful music she had ever heard. It filled her head, so sweet that nothing else mattered. There were no thoughts, only the enticing sounds of the melody.

She knew then it was safe.

Miranda stepped through what remained of the doorway, walking into the burning building.

She took in the changes all around her. The elegant drapes, thick velvets in rich shades of blue and red and gold, were alive with flames. The lush fabric, tattered and charred, disappeared before her eyes as the fire reduced it to ash.

The few pieces of furniture were similarly aflame. The hand-painted designs on an antique table melted from the heat, the intricate pattern merging into swirls of brown. The velvet couch in the small library was an orange and yellow sun. The Oriental carpet was dotted with flame, burning languorously.

She passed through the ballroom. The marble floor was covered with ash and charred pieces of wood that had fallen from the ceiling. Giant flames crackled and spat as they swallowed up the walls. The colors on the hand-painted murals were melting, the fine pastel shades and the darker hues running together as the pictures on the walls dissolved.

The heat in the sealed-up room was so intense that the glass panes in the French doors suddenly shattered, one after another in rapid succession. Through the openings shot blasts of cold air. Already the flames moved out to the garden, spread rapidly by the wind.

Miranda stood in the middle of the ballroom, watching with fascination, separate from the overwhelming destruction yet at the same time a part of it. She felt no sadness, only resignation. This was simply the way it was meant to be.

She understood now that Cedar Crest did not matter. It could not go on; it *should* not go on.

It was Garth that mattered.

He's in there! Up in the tower! Virginia Swensen's

words echoed through her head. Yet the voice she heard was not the woman's. It was a sweeter voice, a guiding voice that wanted to help.

Miranda had never been to the tower, had not even been aware that one existed. Still, she knew precisely what path to follow to get to it.

Enveloped by that same serenity, the same fascination over the sight of Cedar Crest aflame, she floated down long corridors, through rooms and hallways and passages that up until now had gone unexplored. Everywhere she saw destruction, the decaying finery that after decades was finally giving way to the merciless flames, giving way with a sort of relief.

Passing through the kitchen, through a back corridor and around a corner, she found herself at the bottom of a circular stairway. It was made of thick gray stones, winding upward through a narrow passageway.

Go to him, Miranda.

The heat from the fire grew more and more intense as she began her ascent. The sharp crackling noises filled her head, the smoke teased her nostrils. Yet without fear she lifted her feet over and over and over again, climbing upward. She went up forty, fifty, sixty steps, high above the rest of Cedar Crest, not stopping even to catch her breath as she made her way up the seemingly endless spiral. As she walked she clutched the banister, a simple wooden rod that followed the curve of the passageway.

At the top she saw a window, a small circle opening onto the night. Through it shined the light of the moon, illuminating the face of the lone man standing proudly at the top of the tower.

"*Miranda!*" Garth cried. "You came! How did you—"

"Sh-h-h-h." She held her finger to her own lips, then reached over and tenderly placed it against his. "We're safe."

"No, Miranda. We're not safe." He gestured toward the window. "They want me dead. They've come to destroy not only Cedar Crest, but me as well."

"They will not destroy you."

"How can we ever get out—"

"Trust me, Garth." Her voice was calm, nearly a whisper. "I'll lead you to safety. I know the way."

He began to protest, then stopped. Instead he wrapped his arms around her, pulling her tightly against him.

"Miranda, my love!" he cried.

She pulled back, looking at him quizzically. And then she smiled, her entire body infused with a wonderful warmth.

"You love me," she said simply.

"Oh, yes. I never stopped loving you!" Sobbing, he rested his face against her shoulder. "Can you ever forgive me? I only wanted to protect you. I thought it was the only way. . . .

"It was never true, Miranda. Not any of it. I was so afraid, so filled with self-loathing. . . . I had to lie. I had to pretend I no longer cared for you. Don't you see that I had no choice but to send you away?"

"Just say the words, Garth. Let me hear them."

"I love you, Miranda. I love you now, and I'll love you forever. I never stopped. I never will stop."

"Oh, Garth!" She held him tightly against her, their two hearts beating in time.

She could feel her strength rushing into him, and his into her. The energy between them was suddenly so great they both understood nothing could get in its way.

"Oh, Miranda!" he cried. "Now we'll find out if our love is strong enough."

She looked deep into his blue eyes, feeling her own fill up with tears. "It *is* strong enough, Garth. Strong enough to fight even this. You've always said that all you wanted was for me to have faith. I now have that faith. And you must have it too."

She took him by the arm and led him down the stone staircase. The passageway was so narrow they had to walk separately, Miranda in front with her hand stretched out behind her, clasping Garth's. The banister had caught fire so that two streams of flames flanked them as they made their descent.

At the bottom of the staircase, Miranda spotted a door. It had not yet caught fire.

"This door leads to the basement," she said.

"Yes. But they have Cedar Crest surrounded. I could see through the tower window. We can't get out through—"

"There's a secret passageway. It goes underground, under Cedar Crest and out into the forest."

"How do you know?"

Glancing at Garth over her shoulder, Miranda said simply, "I know."

Garth nodded. "My grandfather must have had it built when he designed Cedar Crest," he said.

"Yes," Miranda agreed. "He must have feared this same fate."

The basement was dank, the smell of rot and mildew assaulting her nostrils as she climbed down one more flight of uneven steps. No light got in down here, and she made her way by feeling the walls, their stone surfaces cold and rough against the palms of her hands. Yet she walked with confidence through the passageway snaking through the basement.

She and Garth stopped when they came upon a single candle, barely an inch tall, on the floor. Its light was pale, its flame threatening to go out at any second. But its purpose was clear.

"This is the place," Miranda said.

Already she was pressing her hands against the wall, looking for a way to move the heavy stones, searching for the way out. She felt no fear, no uncertainty, as she moved her hands along the wall.

She never doubted that she would be shown the way.

Suddenly she heard a click. A large piece of the wall sprang forward, moving easily to one side. Beyond was a large dark space, seemingly reaching back forever.

"The secret passageway!" Miranda cried.

"Let's hurry."

Garth led the way, crouching down to keep from hitting the low ceiling. He grasped the small candle in his hand, but with little air it went out after he had traveled less than ten yards. Miranda followed close behind, her hand pressed against his back. She, too, walked hunched over.

They walked through the dark, through the silence, through the stagnant air of the passageway. No sounds from overhead got through the stone tunnel. She did not know how far the passageway stretched; she knew only that it was their only hope, their only chance for escape.

Never for a moment did she stop believing that the narnauks would lead them out of danger.

The air was cold, and more than once Miranda suddenly felt the fine stickiness of a spiderweb across her face. Occasionally a scratching sound broke the heavy silence as a small animal, burrowing inside the damp tunnel, scurried back to its home, mistrustful of the intruders. Still she felt no fear. Garth's hand, clasped against hers, was warm and comforting. She could hear his breaths, heavy yet calm. Taking small, careful steps, walking through the dark without knowing where she was headed, what she passed, she was guided simply by her faith in the good spirits . . . and her love.

All of a sudden something stung her eyes. She snapped them shut, then opened them slowly. Miranda realized that what had irritated them was a tiny beam of light, far off in the distance.

"Garth!" she cried, her heart racing. "We've made it! We've reached the other end of the passageway!"

He quickened his pace. She, too, walked faster, still keeping her shoulders hunched and her head bent, her legs now moving with as much speed as they could. The beam of light grew larger and larger, a circle in the distance that pulled her toward it. It seemed terribly bright after the pitch-blackness of the tunnel, but still she stared right into it, unable to look away.

And then they were surrounded by it. It was the light of the moon, nearly full, as it shined down from high above. Emerging from the tunnel, through a rocky cave, Miranda found herself in the middle of the woods.

"Do you know where we are?" she asked Garth, standing in the forest, blinking.

"Yes," he replied. "I know this place. We're far enough from the house that they won't find us here."

Miranda suddenly realized how exhausted she was. Taking Garth by the hand, she led him to a grassy spot, where she sank down.

Lying beside her, Garth reached over and gently pushed the hair back from her face.

"You saved me," he said, his voice awed.

"No," she said. "Our love saved you."

She studied his face, wanting to savor the way he looked, wanting to remember this moment forever. His skin, streaked with soot, glowed, and his blue eyes burned with intensity. Never had he looked more handsome. Never had she felt more at one with him.

Never had her heart been filled with so much love.

CHAPTER 19

"Where will you go? What will you do?"

Standing in the forest with Garth, clutching his hands tightly in hers, Miranda couldn't bring herself to let him go. She knew she had to; all around them, the pastels of dawn streaked across the sky. The safe cloak of nightfall was vanishing. In the harsh light of day, she knew he wouldn't be safe.

He had no choice but to hide, to call upon the forest to shelter him one more time, just as it had done so many times before.

Far beyond, against the horizon, she could see the smoke snaking upward from what remained of Cedar Crest. A burning smell filled the air, the pungent odor stinging her nostrils.

It was gone. Cedar Crest, once magnificent, was now nothing more than rubble and ashes and charred stones. Only the memory remained.

Yet this was how it had to be.

"I'll be all right," Garth assured her, his blue eyes filled with warmth and love. "The time is growing near, Miranda. Soon, soon . . ."

She nodded, swallowing hard.

He glanced upward, toward the mountains. "I'll keep hidden, up in the densest part of the woods. No one will find me there."

"They think you died in the flames," Miranda said, her voice hoarse. "They think we both did. They won't come looking for us anymore."

He kissed her with more intensity and passion than ever before and then slowly drew away, squeezing her hands tightly. "No. We're safe from them. Now we have other foes to fight."

She watched him head toward the mountains, not looking away until he'd disappeared into the thick growth of trees, no longer visible even to her. And then she turned toward home.

Miranda was exhausted, her great fatigue making even traveling through the familiar terrain of the forest difficult. She longed for the safety of home. The warmth of a steaming shower, the comfort of her own bed . . . she felt she could sleep forever.

Yet she knew she could not. First she had to tell her parents that she was all right, that she had escaped the burning flames of Cedar Crest. Then she needed to rest, to gather up her strength. But the ordeal of the night before had merely been a prelude.

The real battle, she knew, was still to come.

Now is the time.

Miranda awoke from a deep sleep with that thought lodged firmly in her mind. Or maybe it hadn't been merely a thought. Perhaps it had been a phrase spoken aloud, whispered in her ear as she slept, designed to lure her out of her state of unconsciousness and into action.

Within seconds she was completely awake. She snapped her head to the side, anxious to see her alarm clock.

Four o'clock, the glowing letters read.

Four A.M. The hour of the wolf.

Through the window shined a cold, silvery light. The full moon dominated the sky, declaring that this was the night of the winter solstice. Since parting from Garth she had spent the hours alternating between sleep and restlessness. Now, finally, the time had come.

The moonlight bathed Miranda's bedroom with its brightness. Glancing around, she saw how it glinted off the necklace she'd left lying on the dresser, shooting sparkles off the silver chain that linked the tiny figures of animals hand carved from colored stones. The owl, the whale, the eagle, the frog . . .

The wolf.

The moonlight highlighted the Native American mask, propped up on the chair. Tonight it looked particularly eerie, with the beaklike nose, the empty, unseeing eyes, the snarling mouth with its two rows of crooked teeth. The darkly colored feathers and the gnarled twigs and pieces of bark that were nailed along the edges heightened its evil appearance. Yet it was the horns that stood out the most, the glaring orange paint that covered the two sharp protuberances picking up the light so that they glowed.

The moonlight reflected off the knife, lying on the night table beside Miranda's bed, sparks flying off the razor-sharp edge of the metal blade.

The handle was illuminated, as well. The eyes of the light-colored wolf, White Foot, appeared blue. The eyes of Second One, deeply embedded in its dark fur, glowed red.

Lying in bed, Miranda took it all in. Adrenaline pumped through her body, driven by her pounding heart. Yet despite the tension that gripped every muscle, she experienced an incredible sense of lightness. Of energy.

Of power.

Now is the time.

The thought propelled her out of bed.

The floor was cold beneath her bare feet. A sudden gust of wind from the open window sent her white nightgown billowing about her ankles.

Miranda was only vaguely aware of the cold. Instead she concentrated on the mission that lay ahead of her.

Instinctively she knew what to do.

She went over to her closet. With great impatience she reached past the contemporary clothes, far into the back. When her fingers touched the soft velvet of the long dress, her costume from *Saint Joan*, she pulled it off the hanger.

This was the dress she must wear. The dress of a great heroine, Joan of Arc, carrying out a sacred mission. The dress Miranda had been wearing when she first discovered Garth was a werewolf.

Pulling the dark red bodice snugly over her torso, she was struck by the importance of what she was about to do. She was simultaneously reminded of the danger that lay ahead—and the possibility of failure.

The idea of fighting the final battle and losing, she knew, was too devastating even to contemplate.

Miranda glanced into the mirror, studying the earnest expression of the young woman reflected there. She saw tension in her face, taut lines around her mouth, and a remarkable intensity in her dark eyes. It was the face of a girl about to stand up to the most formidable power, to pit her will, her commitment, her strength, against that of evil.

Staring at her own reflection, she wondered if she would ever again stand in this room, looking into this mirror.

Miranda didn't dare dwell on that thought. Instead she turned to the tasks at hand. With mechanical movements she fastened the necklace around her neck. Next she picked up the mask, tucking it under her arm. Then she grasped the knife, wrapping her fingers tightly around the handle.

Stealthily, quietly, she glided down the stairs. She hesitated in the front entryway, wondering if she should stop for a jacket. Miranda knew intuitively that, tonight, she would not feel the cold. Instead she would be protected by that same warmth that had shielded her before, a warmth so great, so all-encompassing, that even the frigid December night would be no deterrent.

Armed with this knowledge, she flung open the front door and stepped out into the darkness.

The wind whipped the folds of her red velvet gown around her legs as she walked. Her hair streamed behind her. Each gust of wind energized her, pushing her onward.

She knew she would find Garth in the forest. There, in the same woods in which the werewolf had once hunted, under the same full moon that had lighted his way, the saga of the Gautier family would finally be resolved.

Still clutching the knife, the tribal mask at her side, Miranda entered the dark enclave of towering trees. Tonight no comfort awaited her here, no serenity cloaked her in its calming embrace. Instead she sensed a terrible turmoil. She heard it in the wind, moaning like the plaintive wails of souls longing to be put to rest. She felt it in the air, chilled not only by the iciness rising off the ocean, but by something else . . . something undefinable, something rooted in a world other than her own.

She could feel it in her own restlessness, the anxiety that gnawed at her, the knowledge that now her love for Garth and her faith in herself would be put to the ultimate test.

She would either triumph . . . or admit defeat.

She walked through the woods, her course unwavering, heading toward the clearing near the cliffs. When she reached the spot directly above Devil's End, she stopped. Behind her was the forest, shrouded by the night. In front of her, far below, were the crashing waves of the Pacific Ocean, swirling around the sharp, merciless boulders of Devil's End. Standing at the edge of the cliff, the wind blowing through her hair, furiously whipping at the folds of red velvet cascading to the ground, she remembered this moment.

Her dream.

Suddenly she turned. A strange noise had caught her attention. In the clearing behind her, illuminated by the bright light of the full moon, she saw two wolves. The two giant animals growled as they crouched opposite each other. Their eyes were locked, hatred glinting in both the pale eyes of the white wolf and the dark eyes of the black wolf.

Miranda's heart pounded as she realized that these two wolves, these two werewolves, were evil Second One and his son, White Foot.

Angrily they faced each other, teeth bared and muscles tensed. Second One suddenly darted forward. With quick, agile movements, White Foot jumped backward, then lowered his head and snarled viciously.

Miranda watched, fascinated but not at all surprised. This battle, she knew, the fight between the good spirits and the bad, had continued for hundreds of years.

One, and only one, would emerge as the victor.

And then her attention shifted. Someone else—*something* else—had come into the clearing.

A golden beast appeared at the edge of the forest, moving silently, keeping himself apart from the other two wolves. Once again, Miranda experienced no surprise.

"Garth," she called, her voice soft.

The werewolf raised his head. Their eyes met. In the moonlight she could see their blue color. Her heart lurched. In those eyes, she could see his agony. His longing.

Looking through them, she could see into his very soul.

She did not see the werewolf. Instead, she saw Garth.

Her Garth. The man she loved.

Yet she knew what she must do.

Miranda was acutely aware of the sounds of the night that surrounded her. The loud crashing of the waves far below, the violent swirls of deep water. The rustling of the evergreens, swaying in the wind. The growling of the two werewolves embroiled in their ongoing battle.

Yet she paid them little heed. She was too absorbed in her own feelings, so powerful, so overwhelming, she wondered how she would ever live through this night.

I can't! a voice inside cried. *I can't do it!*

Yet she knew she had no choice.

Pain tore at her heart. Tears streamed down her cheeks. She tasted their saltiness as they flowed over her lips, parted as she silently mouthed a plea.

No! The word echoed through her mind, over and over again. *There must be another way!*

She waited, desperate for the narnauks to make their presence known. To infuse her with power, to cloak her with their warmth, to carry her through the horrible motions she knew she had to perform. Yet there was nothing.

She was alone.

And then, in a flash of comprehension, she understood that the narnauks had brought her this far. The rest, she had to accomplish on her own. Somehow, Miranda had to reach deep inside and find the strength to lift the curse herself.

That strength, she knew, was rooted in her love for Garth—a love so pure, so unselfish, so true, that it made anything possible.

She closed her eyes, shutting out the night, instead picturing Garth. His face filled her mind. There was nothing else but him.

Suddenly she felt infused with power. It washed over her, energizing her body and lifting her spirit.

Yes, she thought. *I can do it. The power is mine.*

Miranda took a step toward the giant wolf.

She was surprised that he did not react with fear. Instead, in his blue eyes she could see the love. She could see the trust. The part of the werewolf that remained Garth, the part that even the evil power could not touch, had no reason to fear her.

His eyes remained fixed on hers as she donned the mask. He did not flinch as she stepped toward him, her movements hesitant. He did not even wince as she raised her right arm, her fingers tightly clasped around the handle of the knife.

Miranda's arm throbbed as she held it poised in midair. Her heart was pounding so hard she feared it would burst. An energy unlike anything she had ever before experienced rushed through every part of her body.

Yet through it all she felt a sense of serenity. She knew precisely what she had to do. Even more, she knew it was what she was destined to do.

And then, in one swift motion, she brought her arm down. She felt the sharp blade pierce the skin of the werewolf with ease, cutting deeply through the muscular flesh. Immediately a red gash appeared in the ruff of his neck.

Once near the head, the dwelling place of the mind.

The beast let out a yelp, one that rose from deep inside his chest. In his eyes, she could see the terror.

Miranda could feel his pain as if it were her own. She could feel his fear. Above all, she felt his sense of betrayal.

Her heart felt as if it were breaking in two. But still she went on, again raising the knife, spotted with his blood, into the air. Once more she plunged the knife inside the werewolf's flesh, this time cutting him in the side, just above his ribs.

The second time in the side, the center of the body.

The werewolf opened his mighty jaws, letting out a howl.

Behind him, the struggle continued, the two

massive beasts fighting their enraged battle. Ugly snarls rose up, growing more and more angry.

Miranda barely dared glance in their direction. Instead she drew the knife back again.

The third time in the heart, which houses the soul.

Miranda plunged the knife into the golden werewolf, this time aiming directly for his heart.

As she did, a great roar of thunder rose up from the center of the earth. A flash of lightning lit up the sky. In that moment of bright illumination, Miranda saw the white wolf pounce, its powerful jaws clamping around the neck of the dark wolf. Second One let out a cry so piercing, so full of pain, that Miranda shuddered.

And then she saw him creep backward, head down and ears flattened in defeat. He slunk away, moving closer and closer toward the edge of the cliff.

White Foot followed, easing toward the darker wolf but keeping his distance.

Then Second One reached the edge of the cliff. Far below, at the bottom of the sharp, rocky incline, lay Devil's End. The rushing waters, swirls of black and dark green, looked particularly menacing as Miranda glanced over. The boulders protruding from the sea were sharper and more ominous than usual.

She was hypnotized by the view down below. The rhythmic motion of the waves, swelling up, rising higher and higher, then erupting into a burst of white foam as they shattered against the jagged points of the massive boulders . . .

And then, suddenly, her attention shifted. White Foot lunged toward Second One in an abrupt and unexpected motion. The black wolf took a step backward—and tumbled off the cliff, plummeting downward.

Miranda ran to the cliff's edge, horrified as she watched the dark waters of Devil's End swallow up the once fearsome animal. A crash of waves and he was gone, disappearing into the sea . . . lost forever.

She turned, surprised by the sense of lightness that now surrounded her. The terrible feeling of doom had been lifted from the cliff's edge and the forest that surrounded it.

She wasn't at all surprised to discover that White Foot had vanished.

She stood motionless for a few moments, expecting to feel the presence of their spirits. Yet neither the heaviness of the evil narnauks nor the positive energy and warmth of the good narnauks were present.

A feeling of great relief washed over her. Was it possible that it was over?

"Miranda."

There was a question in Garth's voice as he came up behind her, grasping her shoulders gently. Turning, she saw that he was standing behind her, the same question that had been in his voice echoed in his eyes.

Gone were all traces of shapeshifting. Even though the moon was full, even though the blanket of night still surrounded them, he was in human form. He had no wounds. There was only a strong young man who stood before her, his golden curls disheveled, his mouth tense, his blue eyes clouded. He was a man, not a beast.

She understood then that the spell had been broken.

"It's over," she said, her voice a hoarse whisper as she encircled his neck with her arms. She drew him close, resting her head against his muscular shoulder.

"Yes." Wrapping his arms tightly around her waist, he leaned forward and kissed her hair. "It's finished."

"Oh, Garth!" She collapsed against him, all the tension of the night suddenly overwhelming her.

"Are you all right, Miranda?"

"Yes."

Drawing away, she raised her eyes to study him. Finally, he was the man he was meant to be.

Miranda could feel tears welling up in her eyes. Gently she placed her palms on his cheeks, cradling his face in her hands. Gazing into his blue eyes, so clear, so filled with love, she spoke, her voice a hoarse whisper.

"Now we can begin."

About the Author

Cynthia Blair, author of books for both adult and young-adult readers, has published more than thirty novels. She grew up on Long Island, New York, and earned her B.A. from Bryn Mawr College. After four years of working in New York City, she began writing full time. She currently lives on Long Island where she, like Miranda, loves spending time outdoors.

Sweet Goodbyes

A wonderful series of heart-rending stories that will make you cry. Ordinary high-school girls are suddenly forced to cope with a life-threatening illness. Things will never be the same again, as each girl fights to survive...

Please Don't Go
Losing David
Life Without Alice
My Sister, My Sorrow
Goodbye, Best Friend
The Dying of the Light

All at £2.99

Sisters
by Marilyn Kaye

Although the four Gray sisters are close in age, they are very different in character. Phoebe, aged 11, is the baby, a little girl who refuses to grow up. Daphne, 12, is shy and quiet and happy that way – if only her elder sisters would let her be. Cassie, 13, is beautiful, popular and selfish, while Lydia, 14, is an idealistic rebel, whose strong beliefs sometimes land her in trouble. Such different personalities are bound to disagree, but when trouble comes, each knows she can turn to the others for help.

Phoebe	**£2.99**
Daphne	**£2.99**
Cassie	**£2.99**
Lydia	**£2.99**

Order Form

To order direct from the publishers, just make a list of the titles you want and fill in the form below:

Name ....

Address ....

....

....

Send to: Dept 6, HarperCollins Publishers Ltd, Westerhill Road, Bishopbriggs, Glasgow G64 2QT.

Please enclose a cheque or postal order to the value of the cover price, plus:

UK & BFPO: Add £1.00 for the first book, and 25p per copy for each addition book ordered.

Overseas and Eire: Add £2.95 service charge. Books will be sent by surface mail but quotes for airmail despatch will be given on request.

A 24-hour telephone ordering service is avail-able to Visa and Access card holders: 041-772 2281